Margaret Sutton Briscoe

Perchance to Dream

And other stories

Margaret Sutton Briscoe

Perchance to Dream
And other stories

ISBN/EAN: 9783744748483

Printed in Europe, USA, Canada, Australia, Japan

Cover: Foto ©Andreas Hilbeck / pixelio.de

More available books at **www.hansebooks.com**

"PERCHANCE TO DREAM"

AND OTHER STORIES

BY

MARGARET SUTTON BRISCOE

NEW YORK
DODD, MEAD AND COMPANY
1892

University Press:
JOHN WILSON AND SON, CAMBRIDGE, U.S.A

My Mother and Closest Friend:

WHO IS IDENTIFIED WITH EVERY LINE IN THIS BOOK,

WHICH I DEDICATE TO HER.

CONTENTS.

INTRODUCTORY NOTE.

THIS volume of stories, put forth with diffidence and in modesty of spirit, stands in no need of an introduction. A new writer can be introduced only by her work. It is entirely natural, however, that Miss BRISCOE should desire to interpose the word of a friend between herself and a public to whom she speaks for the first time. Fortunately that public is not the many-headed monster which it has sometimes been represented; it is, rather, a very well-disposed public, eager to be interested and ready to welcome every new-comer who cares more for excellence than for reputation. The name on the titlepage of this volume is not entirely unfamiliar, since it has appeared in the pages of the "Christian Union," "Harper's Young People," "The Overland Monthly," and other periodicals.

HAMILTON W. MABIE.

NOTE.—Special acknowledgment is made to Messrs. HARPER & BROTHERS for their permission to reprint, from their "Young People," the story, "Die, Which I Wont."

"PERCHANCE TO DREAM."

"PERCHANCE TO DREAM."

"SPREAD yourself out, Charles," said Mr. Gordon; "fill up as many seats as you can. Your aunt thinks it disloyal to the children to take any leaves out of the table,—so I sit at one end of the deserted board, and she at the other. We can bow to each other, and call something across occasionally."

"You must come often and help us out, you see, Charles," said Mrs. Gordon, smiling, and turning her still beautiful face toward her nephew. "Albert, you should not laugh at your wife's sentiment."

Mr. Gordon was an elderly man, high-featured and distinguished-looking, with clear, brown eyes and clean, olive skin, and a soldier-like alertness of bearing. His white hair, which rioted over his head in crisp curls, lent a further air of vigour to his appearance.

There was a sense of rest and repose about his uncle's home which always soothed Charles Gordon. His presence there was no unusual event, and his place at table was always set, although he had occupied it but little of late. He was strikingly like his uncle in feature. As his self-control relaxed somewhat in this congenial atmosphere, a strained expression of underlying pain now and again crossed his face, and the look of age which then accompanied it brought out this resemblance more strongly.

The servant was filling the wine-glasses by the three plates, and Mr. Gordon raised his to his lips. As Charles bent forward and closed his forefinger and thumb about the stem of his glass, there was a deliberate air of defiance in his action, simple as it was. When he set down his empty glass, he looked steadily across the table at his uncle; the same defiant spirit showed in his eyes, and something not unlike anger tinged his expression.

Mr. Gordon appeared unconscious of all this, but a few moments later he motioned to the servant, who refilled the glass. Charles watched him do so, yet did not immediately touch the contents; his attitude relaxed. There was never anything which jarred upon him here. There was no place just like it; nothing was ever hurried. Dinner meant a pleasant meeting to be lingered over, while the day's gleanings of interest were spread out on the board; and none of the wonted customs were dropped with the dropping away of the younger branches.

Mrs. Gordon rose as usual after dinner, and left her husband with his nephew, as she had been accustomed to leave him with his sons. Charles opened the door for her; and as she passed him she laid her hand lingeringly on his shoulder, with a kind smile. She was not a demonstrative woman, although a tender one; Charles was surprised and touched by the caress. He walked back to the table, and sat down thoughtfully,—his legs stretched out before him, his hands thrust in his trousers' pockets; his face in repose was not happy, and older than his years warranted.

Mr. Gordon had drawn his chair back also; he was sitting with one arm resting on the table, his eyes fastened on the young man's face.

"You are very like me, Charles," he said; "more so than any of my own sons."

Charles flushed, as he looked up.

"You could have said nothing which would have given me more pleasure," he answered quickly.

There was an unaffected genuineness in his voice, and the boyishness of his smile softened his face wonderfully.

"It is a great pity that your own father died when he did," Mr. Gordon went on, — "a pity for both you and your mother."

The gentleness which had come to Charles Gordon's face vanished.

"I saw my mother's carriage leave the door as I came in," he said harshly; "she has you to come to with complaints in her trials."

"Yes, she has me to come to; but it is not quite the same, Charles."

"No," answered Charles; "it is not quite the same."

He took his hand from his pocket, and raised his glass to his lips. Across the rim his eyes were miserable, angry, and defiant.

Mr. Gordon's eyes met them calmly. When the glass was set down empty, he pushed the bottle of wine across the table in silence. Charles lifted it; but his fingers trembled a little so that the glass overflowed. He muttered an apology, thrusting his hand again into his pocket, and staring moodily before him.

"You are not only like me in feature and disposition," said Mr. Gordon, "but your temptations were mine, also. Sometimes I feel that I am living over my youth in yours; it has drawn you very closely to me, my boy."

Charles looked across the corner of the table at his uncle, his brows drawn together in a frown of surprise.

"It is very strange," said Mr. Gordon, reflectively; "there may be a difference in one way. I had no excuse whatever; perhaps you have."

A dark flush swept over the younger man's face; he shrank for a moment, as if a sensitive wound had been touched, then drew himself up slightly and raised his head, waiting.

Mr. Gordon was tipping his empty glass up and down, watching the little rivulets formed by the few remaining drops as they ran together.

"It is very strange," he repeated; he glanced up suddenly, with a direct question. "Has any one ever told you how nearly I made a miserable wreck of my life?"

Charles had no need to answer; the incredulous wonder which he knew his face must express, seemed answer sufficient.

"I was not thoroughly brutish,—or I thought that I was not,—not continuously so, at all events; but I ate of the husks which swine do eat, and found them palatable."

There was a long silence.

Charles closed his eyes, and opened them again; there were throbbing pulses in his head. His old landmarks seemed confused or gone; he tried to recollect how he had spent the hours before ringing his uncle's doorbell, and began to wonder if he had a right to be there at his aunt's table. He wished his brain were a little less benumbed, that he might know. The uncertainty troubled him; but he thought he had not come to that yet in his efforts to forget a form and face and voice which would not be forgotten. He felt that he had now forfeited even the right to this memory; yet he began living over again, for the thousandth time, that past with its dear associations.

"Have you ever noticed the peculiar tenderness and peace in your aunt's face, Charles?" Mr. Gordon was saying.

"Yes," answered Charles, rousing; "but I have always thought her the most beautiful woman I ever saw."

"She was considered wonderfully beautiful when I married her; she had just those same cameo-like features and the superb carriage of the head which she has now. But there was none of that beauty of expression which is now hers; my wife was the essence of high breeding and self-control. I thought that I was in love with her,—and I was, in a way. To-day, as I sit at the head of my table and look down its length at her, I can laugh at the idea under my gray hairs; I was proud of her. It was in my power to adorn her beauty beautifully; and I liked to enter a room with her on my arm, and see heads turn, and eyes follow. That faultless regularity of feature, the statue-like repose which I never saw ruffled, satisfied me perfectly; if there were a flesh-and-blood woman beneath, I never sought to wake her.

"Once, shortly after our marriage, my wife ventured a slight remonstrance — but that is too strong a word —

as to my habits of life. I cut her short on the moment. I was only about your age. After that there was but a prouder lifting of the head, and a drooping of the eyelids to tell me that she even had knowledge of what occurred but too often.

"James Irwin, my wife's elder brother, was living with us then, you know. But I forget, — you know nothing about it; even my children know very little.

"Somehow I am moved to open it all to-night, and lay it before you, Charles, even to that story of my inner life which no one in this world knows, — not even my wife, wholly, although she knows in part. Do I bore you? Shall I go on?"

Charles Gordon, sitting upright and motionless in his chair, stared at his uncle, his eyes wide open and full of perplexity. He passed his hand over his brow, pressing his hot temples.

"Can you ask me?" he replied in a low voice.

"I rather affected the society of older men," Mr. Gordon went on slowly. "There was one circle in which I especially delighted, — a club formed of semi-literary, semi-artistic men, Bohemian to the core, and knowing no law save that laid down by the rules of art or literature. I was the only young man admitted among them, and I was flattered beyond measure at the distinction.

"There was one in this circle who interested me deeply, — no one knew where he came from, or what was his position in life. There were some who insisted that his features were familiar to them; but they were not able to place him further, and it was not well to ask questions in that company. He talked but little, and ate his husks with a curious epicurean deliberation; there was not the flavour of a shred which escaped him.

"At that time I think my ruling passion was a burning, illegitimate curiosity: I would grasp all the secrets of life; I desired to see, to hear, to smell, to taste, to feel, all that body and mind could compass.

"There was something in this man which fascinated and eluded me; not that he avoided me,—rather otherwise,—but I felt baffled when with him. A conviction forced itself upon me that he knew something which I had not yet learned. His was a curious face,—sealed like a mask, totally devoid of feeling; the eyelids generally half-closed, and the eyes beneath opaque and expressionless.

"One evening, when we two sat talking together in a remote corner of the club-room, he asked me abruptly, how I—a mere youth, with the world a ball at my feet—had yet managed to attain that glorious unrest which was mine? I looked up, nettled by the sneer in his voice rather than his words. We were sitting with the corner of the table between us,—very much as you and I are sitting now; he was leaning back in his chair, looking at me from under his eyelids, with a half-mocking smile on his lips.

"'Well-looking,' he went on, 'better married, enough brains, and a plethora of money,—what more do you want?'

"'That which you know,' I replied curtly.

"My companion quite closed his eyes for a moment, and smiled with an enjoyment infinitely irritating.

"'That is the proper spirit,' he began; then with a sudden change, 'but let Time fiddle while we dance.'

"He tossed off the wine in his glass with an exaggerated gesture, then refilled my glass and his own.

"'Let us drink to those provident ancestors who have made your career possible,' he said.

"I checked him, laughing, —

"'No; if they are resting peacefully, let sleeping dogs lie. It was through the Puritan ancestor that the shekels came.'

"My companion set his glass down and laughed; with him there was no sound, yet it was laughter.

"'Who can say that the old psalm-singer is not now standing by,' he said, 'tearing his ghostly hair, and wringing his vaporous hands over the use or abuse of his hoarded gold? Peace to his ashes! May he never walk!'

"'Amen,' I replied. 'But did you never consider what a privilege it might be to walk, — to float through your world, a disembodied spirit, and hear what your friends said of you, yourself unseen?'

"My companion leaned across the table and touched my arm.

"'No; but listen. Did you never consider what a privilege it might be to roam through your world seeing and hearing all that you see and hear, without fully understanding when you are — what shall I term it? — well, a *disemspirited* body? We will call it so for euphony.'

"I looked at him questioningly, but half comprehending.

"'To mingle with one's boon companions," he went on, 'and learn what they said and did, and what you yourself said and did with accuracy. Have you never felt the desire to know — never wished to account for blank hours, which must, from their very nature, have been full of experience?'

"'I never thought of that,' I answered.

"'Think now,' replied my companion, smiling.

"I thought, and with the thinking and the numerous possibilities which opened, the desire was born strongly.

"'It would be profoundly interesting,' I said at last; 'but, alas, impossible. The man is not born who can keep his reason and lose it too.'

"I seemed to catch, for the fraction of a moment, a gleam of light from behind the opaque pupils; the same irritating conviction that this man had a knowledge which was not mine, confronted me.

"'One could assume to have lost his reason,' he answered slowly. 'The effect on outsiders would be the same; and if he be imaginative, he might even deceive himself—but then—no man would carry out the experiment fairly.'

"'What would you call carrying it out fairly?' I asked.

"'Playing the part to the bitter end, should the experiment by chance grow bitter. No; men are cowards, it would be dropped.'

"'That must depend on the man. Do you think there are none brave enough to look the immediate consequences of their own acts in the face when they prove painful?'

"'That,' answered my companion, coolly, 'is Hell. No man will choose to cross a corner of his Gehenna before his time is ripe; be sure of that.'

"The only expression I had ever seen on his face

came there as he spoke: it filled with a cold, mocking scorn.

"'See how even curiosity like yours grows cold as the experiment seems possible,' he said; 'or else your courage.'

"I threw off the slight chill which his words created.

"'You are too serious,' I answered, laughing. 'Do you suppose that what I have faced with Dutch courage, I cannot face with my own? What man has done, man can do; to-night I shall try your experiment. I shall see and hear all that is to be seen and heard, and I shall come out alive on the other side, too.'

"Again it seemed to me that I detected a quick light behind the drooping eyelids.

"'Let us be merry with the jocund grape in earnest,' he quoted lightly.

"'No,' I replied; 'you should not have mentioned a scheme so seductive, did you not wish it tried. After all, I shall only be reproducing yesterday, or anticipating to-morrow maybe. To-night think of me as enjoying a new sensation; that in itself is temptation sufficient.'

"'And if the sensations are not all pleasant?'

"'Is art all pretty?' I interrupted.

"My companion rose and stood before me; he was holding my wine-glass in his hand. It was full to the brim, but not a drop spilled. He looked down into my eyes.

"'Are you in earnest?' he asked scoffingly.

"I felt a strange numbness creeping over me; I was conscious only of the scornful face and the opaque eyes which held mine.

"'Yes,' I murmured hoarsely; 'yes.'

"I felt the glass touch my lips; a finger pressed my brow; I swallowed something which burned like fire, and then — I started up to see two soiled glasses on the table and an empty chair opposite mine.

"That I had been the subject of a mesmerist's trick was the first thought which punctured my stupefaction. My first sensation was naturally indignation; but crowding out everything else, grew a curiosity keener than any emotion I had ever experienced. To try at once that experiment which my strange companion had suggested was the one idea which possessed me.

"Into the hours which almost immediately followed on my resolution, I shall not enter. You may judge of their nature, Charles, partly by experience; it is enough to say that my highest anticipations did not exceed the reality.

"I mounted the steps of my own house afterwards, my brain still rioting and reeling with all that I had seen and heard; I was drunk with excitement, *but with excitement only*. I had in those few hours dipped into the depths of the frailties and brutalities of human nature, and seen it naked with unclouded eyes; I knew myself and those with whom I mingled as years of an ordinary existence could not have taught me.

"There had been no time for reflection; all that my brain could hold had been crowded into it for observation, — a wild Walpurgis night, which I had entered Faust-like. I was still half under the spell of that delirium of experience, when I reached the library where I found my brother-in-law sitting writing; it was his habit to keep early hours, and his presence somewhat surprised me. As I entered the room, thoroughly preoccupied, my foot slipped on the smooth floor, and it was with some difficulty that I recovered my balance.

"James Irwin looked up, then dashed down his pen, advancing toward me excitedly.

"'My God, is it possible! Again, and to-night of all nights!'

"I supposed that my stumble had deceived him; but I would not explain. This was the first time that he had ever attempted open remonstrance, and for the moment I was angered beyond measure.

"Before any further words were possible, there were quick footsteps outside, and my wife entered the room hastily. She was in evening dress; there was an unusual colour in her cheeks, an unusual animation in her movements. I remembered then that I was to have taken her to the ball from which she was now evidently returning; and as I looked at her I almost found it in my heart to regret that I had not been with her.

"She ran past me to her brother's side.

"'He has come, James,' she cried. 'We stopped for him at the train, on the way home, and I have brought him to you. Here he is.'

"The man, who had followed her more slowly, now came forward. He was younger than Mr. Irwin, but the greeting between the two was that of old and valued friendship; both were moved, and hid it under a show of heartiness and laughter.

"Stella stood by, watching them with shining eyes. Her look fell on me, and the change came,—a change which appalled me. The light died out of her eyes with the smile from her lips; an expression of unutterable anguish swept over her features,—an agony so withering, a shame so crushing, that I stood there, thrilled and spell-bound, scarcely believing it the same face. It was all gone in a moment, and in its place was the stately beauty I knew.

"The stranger had turned and looked toward me, half hesitating; Mr. Irwin would not respond. I could see the swelling of her slender throat, as my wife raised her head, like a snow-white flower on its stem; she laid her hand lightly on my arm: —

"'And here is my husband, also, Mr. Alden,' she said; 'Albert, you have heard me speak of James's old friend, — and mine. We must go to the dining-room, now. I have ordered a late supper for you, Mr. Alden.'

"I sat at the head of my table, a haunted and bewildered man, — haunted by the agony of soul which had looked out at me from my wife's eyes, and bewildered because I had no comprehension of what could have evoked that depth of feeling which I did not know existed beneath the cold surface. I had seen what I thought an exquisite statue changed to a living, suffering woman.

"Looking at that stately, gracious hostess sitting there, — graceful, coldly beautiful as ever, — I began to regard the evidence of my own eyes as a figment of my over-heated brain.

"Across the room from me a large mirror was set in the wall; the whole supper-table was reflected in it, — a framed picture, which caught my eye. The white cloth, the twinkling candles, and bright flowers, the shining silver and glass, my wife's slender figure, Mr. Alden bending toward her as he spoke, her brother's listening attitude, and, — was that myself! that being, flushed and wild-eyed, a disordered vision of excitement?

"I could only account for my appearance by supposing that I had thrown myself into my late part too successfully to cast aside the outward show in a moment; but as I saw, an insane impulse — a fleeting impulse only, but even so to my lasting shame — tempted me to assume voluntarily that part which I had unconsciously carried into my home. If that haunting look which I had caught on my wife's face were a reality, I wished to be assured of it. Every instinct repudiated the suggestion as it took form. To carry it out was as far from my intention as light from darkness, and yet, — I was roused to the consciousness that my voice was speaking words which my brain did not originate, which my will did not utter, and I saw on my wife's face that same agony of feature, instantly controlled.

"It was no illusion; my heart leaped up in answer. I thought that I had sprung from my chair to her side, regardless of others; but no, — I was sitting there heavily. A pair of expressionless, opaque eyes seemed looking into mine, a scornful face grew indistinctly about them, with lips that mocked and spoke to me alone: '*Do you forget, or does the experiment grow bitter?*'

"A recollection of the words I had spoken, and the part to which I had vowed myself in the far corner of the club-room, flashed through my brain. My mind answered, not my tongue: '*It did not include this.*'

"The lips laughed the silent laugh once more.

"'*Did it never include this before? Remember, you are only reproducing yesterday, or anticipating to-morrow.*'

"'You lie,' I replied fiercely,—'you lie!' and then was silent, remembering my own words.

"'Look at her!' I cried. 'No; this I have never seen before!'

"Again the lips sneered.

"'*You have, but with unseeing eyes. Has your curiosity grown cold, or your courage?*'

"'Both,' I answered wildly; 'I will not enter my Hell on earth.'

"The face was fading; only the eyes remained,—two threatening stars.

"'*It is too late! You have drained my glass to the dregs.*'

"I started back with a shudder of horror, and woke to the awful knowledge that my will was bound in the circle of another's. With every sense sharpened acutely, sensitive to a breath, a word, an expression, I yet possessed no power to control a self before which I grovelled in a humiliation unspeakable,—a self which I had simulated, and which had not seemed loathsome among its kind.

"I saw James Irwin's hardly repressed indignation, my wife's face white and whiter, that high lovely head still poised proudly, but the heavy eyelids drooping lower and lower. I saw Alden's eyes turning toward her with a yearning tenderness, at which the blood seethed in my veins. And yet this self,—this thing which they thought me, and why not?—was singling him out gayly, eagerly. I had been told often that I was never so brilliant as when freely drinking; that then my brain worked with a feverish rapidity, a scintillating wit, and scathing force; it may have been so. I heard everything that night through a veil of blinding shame.

"Loathing beyond endurance this self to whom it meant madness to be tied, again and again my will wrestled with it, and at each trial the cold, opaque eyes looked on, sucking the life blood of my strength. Each struggle, each failure, left my will weaker, more easy to subdue. The awful moments dragged by; there was not the shaving of the hundredth part of a second of consciousness spared me.

"When human endurance seemed taxed beyond the power of living, my wife rose from the table, quietly and without excuse. She gave no one time to rise with her; yet at the moment of her passing Alden on her way from the room, I saw his face lifted in worshipping pity to hers, and I longed to spring at his exposed throat, to strangle expression out of the face which dared express so much in my very presence; for with a keenness which nothing escaped, I knew that she saw also from beneath those lowered lids. She raised her eyes; her calm gaze met his fully; she passed on and out of the door. No sign of emotion ruffled that marble mask; she was my wife, perfectly loyal to the end,—to herself, and to this creature she thought me.

"I could have fallen at her feet; I was possessed with the desire to follow her, to tell her this was all a hideous mistake, a part forced on me by a devil. With all my frenzied efforts, I found myself still seated motionless listening to the whispers of my companions.

"They had cast aside pretences as the door closed. I had ceased speaking; an intense languor and heaviness were creeping over my body, but hearing and sight were quickened.

"'You should have warned me; you should have spared me this,' Alden was saying, his hand was shading his eyes.

"'Had there been time, I would have prevented your coming. Ah, my friend, if it could have been otherwise!'

"Alden turned away with a quick gesture for silence.

"They spoke together in low voices, oblivious of me; but I was piecing out a conclusion, — fitting a word here and a suggestion there.

"At last Alden rose. 'I shall leave now, and without again seeing her; it would only add to her humiliation. Tell her — no, tell her nothing — what is there to say?'

"They passed from the room into the hallway. Compelled by the force which mercilessly drove me, I staggered after them, and found myself grasping the unwilling hand of the man whose presence in my house I now believed I had both reason and right to question. I was bidding him a farewell odious in its warmth. Powerless to resent the cold contempt of his civility, the fact that the very tones of his voice despised me, I was yet urging his stay with a mad hospitality, while longing for one moment of freedom to dash my fist into the mouth which smiled contemptuously in my face.

"As he turned from me, I reeled back into the folds of a portière which fell before the door of the little withdrawing-room off the hall. I caught the swinging curtain and stood in the open doorway, half hidden, maddened with disgust, shuddering at this self which wrapped me like a noisome serpent; then came a realization which brought me the calmness of despair. This disgust, this horror, were new to me and to me only; not new to others,—not new to her.

"My wife was coming down the stairway. The two men glanced at each other, and then waited for her in silence.

"She came toward them, smiling through her pallor.

"'You would have gone without seeing me?' she said with gentle reproach; she held out her hand as she spoke.

"I saw Alden take it reverently in his; I heard his voice break as he bade her farewell, turning hastily away. The door closed, and with its closing, her hands hid her face.

"'You have broken his heart among you, and now your own,' said James Irwin's voice, bitterly.

"I staggered into the room behind me and sank into a chair.

"If my wife's heart were mine, I had never questioned; besotted with self, I had asked only if I were satisfied. And I had been satisfied; I had not asked for more. Why now this indiscribable sense of injury and loss? My chair was turned with its high back toward the door, and presently I heard her footsteps behind it; she had entered the room and was coming forward, her eyes fixed before her, her face speaking of infinite regrets and sadness to my jealous eyes. She paused with her hand on the back of my chair, not seeing me; then she looked down. Her hand caught the chair for support; she trembled and quivered, but not more than I in my torture of inaction. What did I represent to her at this moment as she looked down on me, a mere soulless carcass to the sight? She was bending over me, moaning under her breath,—

"'Oh, my fallen idol!'

"I held my breath to hear her. 'My fallen idol, for those eyes of all others to see your feet of clay!'

"Passionate response surged from my heart to my lips. 'Let me speak to her,' I groaned; but there was no sound. I was struggling, writhing, fighting, but without motion. With a sickening sensation of bodily pain, a gathering gloom closed about me, in which the only break was a gleam of light from behind dull, opaque eyes, half covered with their lids. It was in them that the force which held me lay, against them that every fibre of my body and brain was concentrated in the desperate struggle. I was in an outer darkness where there was only a sound of weeping, of rending sobs, each one beating on my heart and calling me as by name.

"'Let me go to her,' I gasped, soundlessly, again.

"'*Are none brave enough to look the immediate consequences of their own acts in the face?*' whispered a voice like the hissing of a snake in my ear. Drops of sweat stood on my brow; body and soul, held as in a vise, were quivering in every nerve, straining at every muscle. Darkness and death seemed to fall; deep called to deep over my head, and then, above all, piercing and clear, rose a still, small voice:—

"'Out of the Deep have I called upon Thee, O Lord.'

"My lips moved, my tongue loosened; words long strangers to heart and lip burst from me:—

"'Lord, hear my voice!'

"I was at my wife's feet, telling her I scarcely knew what, yet I think in some way she understood and was satisfied.

"We were clinging fearfully together like children. The head which had been so proudly carried through all was bowed on my breast. I was pouring out my repentance and vows in her ear, — vows which have never been broken. When the morning light came into the room through the shutters, we were still sitting there, hand in hand. I threw open the window, and we stood watching the dawn breaking over the housetops, — the dawn of a new day. By its light I first saw that peace and tenderness in my wife's face, and with a new anxiety I marked its pallor. As I hurried her to her room for a few hours sleep, I knew that for myself sleep was impossible. I went out into the streets through the dim, gray light, communing with my soul, which had been born again, full of wonder and thankfulness. Then it was that I dreamed out humbly and with stumbling prayers the life which is now reality, — the life in which you know me, Charles. Only when the working world began to wake, and the shutters to be taken down from the shop-windows, did I turn toward home.

"The gold band which your aunt wears above her wedding ring is a trifle too wide for a guard; I bought it on my way home that morning, and had the date of our true wedding engraved in it. This we call our marriage ring, Charles; and now you know the story of my inner life."

Charles Gordon, sitting in his chair opposite his uncle, gazing at him, motionless and bewildered, started and passed his hand before his eyes, then stared again. In his uncle's place sat a figure which he knew and did not know.

The face was scornful; the eyes half shut and without expression. The figure was dim and shadowy.

"*Have you the courage?*" asked the mocking lips.

He knew the words they spoke by their motion; for there was no sound. Charles felt his heart leap up and then contract. The power of bodily motion seemed gone from him, and in its place was an activity of mind which stretched out before him a panorama of past days and weeks, before which he shuddered and shrank back.

"No," he muttered hoarsely,—"no, no—"

"Has it been so bad as this, Charles?" whispered a sorrowful voice; he thought it the Voice which would not be forgotten.

But now a strange languor was creeping over him through which he could be sure of nothing.

"Has it been so bad as this? Courage, oh, courage! All is not lost!"

The figure in the chair rose and lifted his glass from the table. It was over full until the wine stood like a rounded ball above the rim, yet not a drop spilled.

"*Have you the courage?*" asked the silent lips again.

Charles lifted his eyes heavily to the opaque ones above him.

"I am ready," he answered dully; a quick light gleamed from behind the falling eyelids.

The eyes held his. A shadowy finger rose and pointed to his brow; the glass touched his lips.

With sudden revulsion, and an effort which was like the wrenching apart of body and soul, Charles broke from the torpor which held him.

He struggled to his feet with a hoarse cry of defiance.

"Away with you! I will have none of your mummery. Leave me be to work out my own salvation with my God."

His hand struck down the glass, which fell to the floor with a crash.

"Charles, my dear boy, Charles," said a gentle voice.

Charles Gordon opened his eyes and looked up into his aunt's face. His uncle was standing beside her, and on the floor lay a broken wine-glass, the wine soaking into the carpet.

"Have you been dreaming?" said Mr. Gordon. "We heard your cry upstairs; you were half asleep when I left you."

Charles looked at him silently, a great fear in his eyes. His limbs were shaking and his lips were tremulous.

What part of this had his uncle's voice told him? What part a phantom of sleep?

"Yes," he faltered; "I—I have been dreaming."

His aunt raised her soft handkerchief and wiped away the drops of sweat which stood on his brow; as she did so, Charles saw above her wedding ring a band of gold wider than a guard.

Somewhere,—not in space or in form,—as it were in his mind's eye, there rose before him a scornful face with eyelid's half shut over opaque eyes, and lips which curled in a mocking smile.

Charles closed his hand over his aunt's, clasping it closely. He rose to his feet, facing he knew not what; his voice was trembling and uncertain, but his eyes were fixed steadfastly before him.

"Whether I have dreamed or lived," he said, "it is the

same; I, too, have passed through, and have come out on the other side, not dead, but alive."

"Wake, dear, wake!" said Mrs. Gordon; "Albert, rouse him, he is still dreaming."

Mr. Gordon laid his hands on his nephew's shoulders, and looked searchingly into his face.

"No," he said with a strange smile,—"no, he is awakened."

HOW THE SPIRIT MOVED CYNTHIA.

How the Spirit Moved Cynthia.*

I HAD said to a friend:

"I want to go to a river,—a river in the mountains,—and I want to see new faces. I want to be with people who won't expect anything in return for amusing me,—with simple folk who have simple ideas, or none at all; for I find the society of a perfect fool is the most acceptable to me just now."

"You need hardly leave your native city to seek that commodity," my friend answered.

"Yes; but the city fools catch the cant of the day, and I am so weary of it all."

"I know just what you mean, just what you want, and just where to send you to get it," my friend answered. "I will give you the address of a farm-house in the Virginia mountains where I was fishing last summer. The people there will take you in if you say I sent you; and I think it will meet all your requirements. I should certainly risk it if I were you."

And risk it I did—not without some misgivings.

---

* For the accuracy of this story I cannot answer. It is contrary to every law of the Society of Friends. I can only quote Reuben Grey as an eye-witness, and my authority.

The family proper was small: the old farmer himself, Reuben Grey, — a man of more than eighty years, — his wife Mary, and their adopted daughter Cynthia. Then came, equally a part of the household, Sam, an old negro slave born on the same day as his master.

But the centre and flower of the whole place was Cynthia. Her mother had been a Quakeress who, alone in the world, had somehow wandered into the circle of kindness surrounding Reuben Grey. He had taken her and her child, first to his hearth, and then to his heart. I do not know which was the more large and warm.

The mother had not lived long to enjoy either, and her dying wish was that her child should be brought up in the faith of her forefathers. This the pious Presbyterian couple, who took the poor little waif as their own, had honestly striven to accomplish.

Cynthia was now eighteen years old, and she had been sent to the Quaker settlement regularly every Saturday night, to receive religious instruction from the good "Friends" until Monday morning's duties drew her back to the farm. She was almost too sedate and prim sometimes. She talked little; but what she said was in a voice so round and sweet that I loved to listen to it, even when she was only counting over the eggs for market. She always used the attractive "thee" of her people; and there was about her an intense though soft reserve which kept me doubly interested in her.

Next in my favour stood Sam, — Sam, with a bunch of rags for a coat, one eye in his head, one tooth in his mouth, and a perfectly white goatee growing out of one side of his chin with a crookedness which was irresistible.

Such was the homestead, and so it happened that I came to be standing in the strawberry patch of a run-down Virginia farm, listening to the grumbles of old Sam, who, unconscious of my presence, was picking berries for my supper.

"Cuss Abe Lincoln, cuss Abe Lincoln, I say! had'n bin fer his dern foolishness, I bin a-settin' in Massa's quarters dis day a-doin' nothin'. Ole as I is, an' pickin' berries in dis hot sun! Cuss Abe Lincoln!"

"Oh, Uncle Sam!" I cried.

"Lord bress yer, chile, yer dun scere me to def. Honey, don' never speak to Sam suddint from behin'. I's a-tremblin' all over."

"What makes you so cross to-day?" I asked.

"Mis'ry, chile; mis'ry all down dis side, an' shootin' cross here, an' up de oder side."

He exemplified on his spare person with his thin hand.

"De berry-lines, dey pears to git longer an' longer," he sighed plaintively.

I took pity on him.

"I'll help you pick, if you will promise not to swear at President Lincoln any more."

Uncle Sam possessed, with the rest of his race, a talent for skipping the disagreeable with a calm adroitness which any woman of the world might have envied.

"Yes, honey," he said, coaxingly. "Yes, help pore ole Sam a mite — how's your pretty ma?"

"Quite well," I answered. "And how is your niece? Do you think her husband has really deserted her? I was sorry to hear of her being in trouble."

"Well, not to say 'zactly in trouble, Miss Katrine. Yer see, Ozella, she ain't no fool. Ef a nigger don' wan' her, she don' wan' dat nigger. She ain't cryin' none, naw, indeed; she 's studyin' 'bout Ozella, an' dere ain't no time ter cry. I ain't a-sayin' don' cry ef you 's got plenty o' money, like you is; but cryin' an' starvin' is sompin else. Naw, indeed, honey; be tough wid de times, I says, and Ozella, she feel jes' like me. Dar somebody calling of yer now."

There was a handkerchief waving from a window of the house, which I knew meant that my mother was waiting for me to walk with her. I left the berry patch and walked slowly toward the house, looking, as I did so, with a dreamy enjoyment at the sunny fields and at the clamouring river which ran beside them, — a river which was running swiftly downhill to reach the mountain's base.

There was nothing particularly attractive about the house itself, excepting the negative charm of being almost hidden by creepers and honeysuckle. It stood remote from the main road, so isolated as to make the figure of a man sitting on his horse in front of the yard gate an object of curiosity to me. I was attracted by the fact that the rider possessed a more intelligent face than any I had seen in this part of the world, and that his general appearance was manly and striking. He was talking to the family, who were collected on the porch, and as I drew near said hastily and with evident confusion, —

"It 's to be next Saturday, — to-day week. I hope you will all come, and your guests as well." He hesitated a moment, and then looked wistfully at Cynthia. "Thee will come, will thee not?" he asked.

She only smiled in answer. It seemed to satisfy him, however, for he made his adieux and rode away as I stepped on to the porch.

"I have an invertation to a weddin' for you, Miss Katharine," cried the old farmer, gayly.

"Is that young Nimrod to be married?" I asked.

"His name ain't Nimrod; it 's Richard Rolf. But he 's to be married to the prettiest girl in thirty miles, to-day week."

The prettiest girl in thirty miles! I looked at Cynthia's delicate beauty, and wondered where were his eyes.

"As pretty as a picter," he went on. "She 's town-bred, and not bin here long. Her mother was a Quakeress from the Settlemunt, — like our Cynthy here; but she married a city man, and out o' the faith, so they cast her off. But las' winter she died, the same week as her husband; and then her people they went up to town and got Dora, the onliest child, and brought her down here to upset ev'ry lad in the Settlemunt. All of 'em were buzzin' 'round her. Even Richard, who allays was a stiddy chap, sort o' got crazy 'bout her; and bein' as he has the best farm 'round here, — the Quakers think a heap of them things, — they do say her uncle, Frien' Moore, gave the thing a shove along. They 'll make a fine-looking pa'r. But Cynthy can tell you more 'bout it than I can; they 're her frien's, all belongin' to the Settlemunt — eh, Cynthy?"

"I think thee has told all that I know, Father," said Cynthia, with gentle indifference.

"I ain't got but one thing agin' Richard," continued the farmer, reflectively; "he 's too Quaker. He don't be thee-ing *ev'rybody*, like our Cynthy here — only his kind; but, Lord! he 'd better be a-theeing all over the place than bein' so sot in his ways about the movin's of the Sperit. I never see nobody believe in it like Richard Rolf."

"A fanatic?" I asked.

"I don' know what you city folks calls it. I calls it a fool. Who 's to say which is a-movin' folks to speech, the Sperit or the flesh? But Richard, he believes it 's allays only the Sperit; and nothin' would shake him."

"How old is he?"

"Twenty-seven, and Dora just seventeen. I don' believe in a man marryin' so young myself. It 's too big a risk for the lady, too big a risk. It takes a long time to be sure a man 's settled in his ways. Now, I married at thirty-seven, and I doubted then but I was too young. I kep' feelin' anxious for some years on Mary's account. I might 'a' broke out any time. A lady can't be too keerful."

So saying, the kindly old man wandered off, intent on his farm duties, leaving me with a strong desire to be present at the Quaker wedding.

Sunday had come and almost gone. It was so like any other day on the farm that had I not been told of its presence by my calendar, and observed a palpably clean collar on the master of the house, and one layer less of dirt on old Sam, I should not have known any difference from the week days. The early supper had been eaten, and the "men-folks" were sitting on the back porch, wrapped in clouds of tobacco smoke, and talking on that exhaustless topic, "the wa-ar." It was here as present a theme as if still raging around the pretty homestead. It seemed as if the feeling were to be bequeathed to children's children.

Ah, I could not wonder. On the hillside at the back of the house was the family graveyard. There lay the "ole mistis," with her husband beside her. They had dropped as the sere leaves, not before their time. About their deaths hung no bitter memories; but who can comfort Rachel mourning for her children! In one corner of the graveyard I found a slab of marble; carved on it in rude letters were these simple words, which told their own sad story, —

IN THE SERVICE OF THEIR COUNTRY:

REUBEN GREY died 1862, aged seventeen.

HENRY GREY died 1861, aged nineteen.

FRANCIS GREY died 1861, aged eighteen.

All sons of Reuben and Mary Grey.

"Truly," I thought, "the bitterness of death is here."

I had never heard the names of these children pass the lips of the father or mother, and I need not say that I never alluded to the discovery, which had inexpressibly touched me. On this particular night I felt in no mood for listening to the old soldiers' stories, — they had a tone of sadness, even the jocular ones; so I sought the solitude of the front veranda. I sat down on the steps, basking in the peace and quiet beauty of the night.

The full moon was riding high in the heavens, throwing the shadows of the vines about the porch on the broad flags at my feet. There was just enough soft breeze to make the phantom leaves dance weirdly. The whole place seemed asleep except for the "cluck, cluck," of an uneasy hen who could not settle herself to her mind on the bough of a tree near the porch, where she perversely elected to roost instead of in the comfortable hen-house. The revery into which I had fallen was suddenly interrupted.

"Does thee believe that every one has a soul?"

The voice was Cynthia's, but a harsh note in its usual music and the abruptness of the question made me start and look up hastily.

"Does not your Church teach you that every one has a soul, Cynthia?"

"Oh, yes," she replied indifferently.

"Then why do you ask me such a question?"

She laid her hand lightly on my arm, and drew me to the other end of the porch.

"Look!" she said scornfully. I looked, and smiled as I did so. There, half in the shadow of the old house, stood Ozella, the deserted one,—deserted, but not inconsolable, it seemed, for by her side, and by all signs having proved his power to comfort, stood a new adorer.

I turned away, and sat down upon the steps again, motioning to Cynthia to sit beside me. I was amused by her disgust and desperate earnestness.

"It is not possible, Cynthia," I said, laughing, "that you think faithlessness proves an absence of soul! Why, child, if that were made a sure test, half of the women in the world, I know, would be proved soulless."

Cynthia bent forward, and laid her hand on my arm; through my thin sleeve I could feel that it was burning as with fever. The moon shone full on her face, and I saw its eager look; her lips were parted, a bright spot of colour burned in either cheek, and her eyes, which were of a soft blue usually, looked black and brilliant.

"Thee will tell me," she breathed; "is it so with men also out in the world?"

I looked at her in dumb amazement. Was this the same self-contained little maiden who had waited on us at supper, and whom I had thought more than usually sedate all day? A light broke on me suddenly. I remembered, with a flash of inspiration, the wistful look cast on her by the young Quaker the day before; and I knew also that Cynthia had refused to be driven over to the Settlement on Saturday evening, pleading a headache. And now this outbreak; for so I may call it. Had I fallen on a little tragedy in this mountain fastness? Poor little one! she was so young and tender to have learned already that stern lesson of her sex,—to appear most outwardly composed when her heart was sorest. I wondered *how* faithless this lover had been; and I could not think that Cynthia had given her heart to one wholly unworthy, even with my slight knowledge of her character. All this darted through my brain in a moment; then I suddenly determined—Heaven forgive me!—to play Providence.

"Cynthia," I said, "if a man had given his vows to one woman, and then discovered that another had his heart, do you think he should keep up the mockery of a false faithfulness?"

"But why should his heart change?" she asked quickly.

"How can any one tell? Solomon himself knew nothing of 'the way of a man with a maid.' It might happen, and neither he nor the second woman be to blame."

Cynthia suddenly interrupted me. "Does thee mean to show that there can be any right in the woman who steals what belongs to another, or in the man who lets her?"

"It might be neither a question of stealing nor letting; the discovery might surprise both."

"Thee knows, then, it is the Devil teaching and blinding them. There could be no blessedness in such a marriage; and thee forgets—thee utterly forgets that other woman."

I longed to gather the suffering child in my arms, and soothe her with gentle words and caresses; but this, I knew, would be a cruel kindness.

"No, Cynthia," I answered; "I do not forget the other woman. Her part is a cruelly hard one, but not so hard as it would be if a false sense of honour bound the man's body when it could not bind his soul."

"She would have no wish to bind him; she would only despise them both," said Cynthia, finally.

I passed over the question of the rival woman. "It would not make her despise him if she loved truly, Cynthia; she would learn to understand that he was right."

"Would thee be willing to love so?" asked Cynthia.

"Cynthia, if you are going to do any work to-morrow, child, you 'd best go to bed now."

A heavy step sounded on the floor, and the portly figure of Mrs. Grey showed in the open door; I looked gratefully at her. The interruption was welcome, for I could not quite assure myself that Cynthia's question did not contain a spirit of criticism; certainly I had no answer ready, and my enthusiasm for playing Providence was dashed. Cynthia glided by me like a shadow, leaving me feeling as one might who had torn open a lily-bud and thus caught a glimpse of the golden heart within.

"It 's a beautiful night, Miss Katharine," said Mrs. Grey; "but to-morrow 's wash-day, and I don't like that rim to the moon,—it looks like rain."

Called back thus to earth and mundane matters, I bade my hostess a preoccupied good-night, and sought my room and my bed.

The marriage morning of Richard Rolf dawned bright and beautiful, and found me a strangely excited and interested spectator of the sad little drama going on under my eyes, the existence of which I alone suspected. Cynthia had shown no consciousness on meeting my eyes the morning after her self-betrayal; she neither avoided my look nor sought it, and in just the same manner did she behave regarding my society.

As I have always held that the sin of betraying the secrets of one friend to another paled before the sin of betraying the mood of one day to the mood of the next, I ignored, as Cynthia did, our conversation of Sunday night. I should have grown to think it a dream of my own brain's spinning, had I not seen under Cynthia's eyes those dark rings which betoken sleepless nights, and observed her more than usual silence. Her work was as well and as regularly done as ever; the same gentle sweetness and serenity was hers, at least outwardly. Her silence was unnoticed by the kind farmer and his wife, for she was, as ever, ready to discuss fully any new project on the farm or in the housekeeping. Even now I could hear her talking over plans for Monday's apple-peeling with her adoptive mother as they sat behind me in the wagon, driving over to the Quaker wedding. I had wondered if Cynthia's strength would carry her through this hardest trial; and in my heart, I applauded the dignity and self-control which prompted her to be present.

Sam sat on the front seat beside me, ostensibly driving; but I had long ago taken the reins from his hands. He was idly flicking at the flies on the horses' backs with his stubby whip.

"You see dat," he said, and pointed to a jagged scar

on the near horse's flank. "Dat gemman fren' o' yourn what war here las' year, he done cure dat. What he don' know 'bout hosses ain' wuth knowin'—ef he did fit on de oder side in de wor."

"Which is the other side, Sam?"

"De Yanks, honey," Sam continued, his elbows on his knees, and his woolly white head nodding to emphasize his remarks.

"Young mars, he fit 'em toof and nail, an' lef' me to take keer o' ole mars an' ole miss', an' de young mistis too. 'Sam' says he, 'I leaves you as a kind of gardeen for 'em all,' he says—'a kind of gardeen.' Den he got hisse'f shot in de leg: not in de battle whar de two fust pore chillerns was kilt, but in de one whar little Rube was lef'. Dey never did see him no mo'; we don' know what did come to de chile. Hit all jes' dig ole mistis grave, hit did; but little Rube, dat cut her mos'. When young mars he come home, den I went an' I fit dem Yanks fur more 'n a year."

Oh, Uncle Sam—Uncle Sam, you hoary old sinner! Do I not know your story! Do I not know how you thirsted for "freedom," and how you deserted wounded young mars, ole miss', and all, to cross the lines and get out of Dixie; and have I not seen the pathetic letter which came from the Massachusetts Hospital after the Spring of '65, saying, "Young mars, fur de Lamb's sake, come git Sam. I never run away no mo'."

The cruel New England winter had frozen all love of freedom out of poor Sam's heart, child of the sun as he was; but Sam had his own pleasing little fiction concerning that year of absence, and had told it so often that I think he had taught his feeble brain to believe it.

By such discourse did he beguile the way, until at last the ten miles of wooded road were travelled and the Quaker meeting-house was in sight. It stood a little apart from the Settlement, and was built on the side of a hill so steep that a realization of the tenacity it must require to stick on made me feel tired as I looked at it.

We were among the last arrivals, and had barely taken our seats with the assembled "Friends," when Richard Rolf entered quietly and sought his place among the men on the other side of the aisle.

I stole a look at Cynthia, but she had taken her Quakerdom and wrapped it about her as a garment; I could learn nothing of her feelings from her face. She had looked at Richard when he entered the room, as did the other women, and then cast her eyes down again.

The door soon opened to admit the bride, who walked into the meeting-house between her uncle, Friend Moore, and his wife.

When I saw her, I had to admit, in spite of my jealousy for Cynthia's loveliness, that she possessed a dusky beauty, as perfect a type of its kind as the dreamy face on which I had loved to gaze. There was not enough character in the soft contour of Dora's face; but one gained an impression of a distracting prettiness and coquetry — just the kind of face Hetty Sorrel must have had, I thought. She might have turned older and wiser heads than Richard Rolf's with that seductive grace and softness.

She sat down, nestling close to her aunt's side like a frightened child; it was easy to see that she was a "Friend" by adoption, not birth. Her hands were twisted restlessly together, and her eyelids, which she never raised, fluttered nervously. The utter silence in the room was broken suddenly by a late comer, and then for the first time the bride raised her eyes, and I saw their lovely soft brown; but why, I wondered amazedly, should they dilate and express such helpless terror as they fell on the face of the man who had just entered.

He was standing against the opposite wall — for the room was crowded — and was fixing his eyes upon Dora with an unmistakably stern and threatening expression. That he was "of the world" was shown by his dress; and that the world had left its mark on him was stamped on his features.

But now Richard rose, and, in the quaint Quaker phrases, took Dora for better, for worse. As he finished speaking, the bride rose mechanically; and as she did so, I looked at the man opposite.

He was leaning forward, his gaze fixed on the bride as before, only more intensely, more burningly; and, as though drawn against her will, Dora turned her face to him.

In that moment I was sure I saw her eyes answer his, and the next she tore them away, and, turning from him, opened her lips.

"I, Theodora," she began, then faltered, wavered, and, flinging herself on her knees before her aunt, she clung to her, crying wildly: "I cannot do it! Oh, I cannot — I cannot!"

Friend Moore rose from among the men, and crossed over to her. "Dora," he said sternly, "is thee mad? Thee has heard naught against Friend Rolf?"

"No, no," she sobbed; "but there is something within me that tells me ill of him, and I dare not marry him."

"Dora," began her uncle, still more sternly; but Richard interrupted him.

"Nay, Friend Moore, thee shall not force the maid." His voice was strained and harsh, his face gray, and the veins showed large on his temples, but the composure of the young fanatic was perfect. "If the Spirit condemn me through her, I must bear it as a man may. Who can say how black his own soul's sins are? If mine be so deeply stained that the Spirit warns a pure maid to beware of me, then it is best that I should know the truth."

I heard a quick breath drawn close by me, and my heart gave a great throb as I turned and looked at Cynthia.

She was standing,—the Cynthia of Sunday night. There was the same soft flush on her cheek, the same eager eyes—none of the Quaker cloak left. She was always lovely, but now—heavens, how beautiful she was! Her voice, when she spoke, thrilled me unspeakably; it had the tenderness of a mother to her child, of a woman to her lover.

"Richard, she is deceiving thee; it is not the Spirit moving her. I am as pure a maid as she, and nothing tells me ill of thee; I would not fear to marry thee this hour."

Shaken, trembling, where now was Richard's composure? Striding across the room, he caught Cynthia by the wrists, his glowing face and excited demeanor contrasting strangely with his Quaker garb.

"Cynthia," he whispered almost fiercely, "does thee mean it? Will thee prove it by doing so? I have been as one possessed. Can thee ever possibly forgive?"

"Thee knows it, Richard."

"And thee will really marry me, and now?"

"As thee wills, Richard."

"Then know all present that I, Richard, take Cynthia for my wedded wife."

And almost before we had recovered from the shock of the surprise, the brief religious ceremony was begun and ended, and Richard and Cynthia were man and wife.

"Well, ef dat don' beat all—dat pore pretty chile! I reckon Cynthy won' cry none."

I moved quickly to the kitchen-door when I heard these words the morning after Cynthia's strange marriage.

"What is it, Uncle Sam?" I asked anxiously.

"Dat pore little Dora dun run away, honey," answered Uncle Sam, the news-gatherer.

"Run away?"

"Yes, honey; let herself and her closes down outen der winder las' night."

I began to see light.

"To whom did she let herself down?"

"To dat onery city cousin o' hern. He bin a-hangin' roun' ever sence de chile cum from town. Dey say ole man Moore run him off at las', but he war down to de weddin' onexpected yestiddy; an' now he done got her, and what he gwine to keep her on, de Lord knows. She air as putty as a pigeon, she air; but she carn't fly aroun' a-feedin' of hersel' like dey do. Naw, indeed!"

So this was the spirit which had moved poor Dora. Cynthia had not been mistaken, nor had I been over ready in surprising meaning glances; for that the cousin and the mysterious worldling of yesterday were one and the same I could not doubt. I hoped that he might belie his looks, for the sake of the pretty, rebellious girl; but my heart was too full of Cynthia to think much of Dora's fate.

I felt that I had played a large part, though behind the scenes, in the little drama just enacted; and I was anything but comfortable in my self-imposed responsibility. I knew so little, and I had spoken so strongly. Suppose Richard were really unworthy! I had certainly striven to prove to Cynthia that he was not; but then how could I guess that a new character would be introduced at the last moment, that the actors would throw their lines to the winds and speak according to their own wills, and above all that Cynthia should play so unexpected a part and improvise so amazingly? I longed to know if she were happy, or if she already repented her rash act.

Only once had she shown me her heart; and but once more was I to look into its pure and lovely depths, and then for a moment only.

In a few days I was to leave the mountains forever, and I felt that I could not go without a word of farewell to Cynthia; so the good farmer drove me over hill and dale to her new home. We took many packages with us,—useful household trifles supplied from the pantry of the kind adoptive mother.

That drive will always live in my memory; I can close my eyes now and feel a sense of light and of heat without its enervating warmth, and see the many greens of the trees, and hear the sleepy swish and ripple of the water.

By my side was old Reuben Grey, whose flow of speech needed no rousing of my mind to comprehend, nor any prompting to go purling on as steadily and restfully as the river whose bed we followed.

How I bathed my soul in quiet and nothingness, and how like heaven I thought it!

I noticed idly that for some reason the old man chose to drive with one foot hanging out of the dilapidated buggy. Was it in memory of the departed days of blooded horses, when it was safer to be always ready? I do not know, but he only drew in that wagging foot when fording the river, which we did about a dozen times in our zigzag course. Some of the fords were good, some bad. At the worst, Reuben Grey drew rein and suggested that I should take up a package of biscuits which lay at my feet and put them in my lap.

"And," he added calmly, "ef I was you, I would jest tuck up my feet on the dashboard before we get in the water, for it do come in powerful sometimes."

I took the biscuits into my lap and tucked my feet up on the dashboard. Though the water did not come in, it might have.

"Anyway, we were ready for her," said the dear prudent old man.

At last we reached Cynthia's home, and we found her the same gentle, placid Cynthia; looking at her, who could dream of the slumbering fires within?

"He," she told us, was out on the farm. "He" always means the good man of the house on mountain-tops.

The young wife was gracious and self-possessed, showing us over her thrifty, comfortable house, and never by word or look referring to any of the strange features of her marriage; her gentle dignity was beautiful in its simplicity.

Only in the few moments when Reuben Grey was untying the horse were we alone.

I could stand it no longer. "Dear Cynthia," I cried,

"are you happy? I shall never see you again, and I should like to hear you say so before I go."

She raised her eyes to mine, and I could see that they were full of tears.

"Yes," she said simply; "and I shall never forget thee; for it was thee that made me do it. I could never have said I knew no ill of him if thee had not shown me he had done no ill; thee did teach me to wrestle with myself and my pride, and all my happiness is from thee, under God. He knows I must always love thee."

I took her glowing face in my hands and kissed her without speaking.

I was very silent all the way home,—so silent that my companion inquired anxiously if I were ill.

"No," I thought, "not ill, only awestruck." I had taken a human soul in my hands to play with it, and it was so beautiful it had frightened me.

A CHIP

A CHIP.

JO TALIAFERRO'S father was poor, his father had been poor before him, and his grandfather back of him again. It was in his great-grandfather's days and through his great-grandfather's hands that the money had slipped away from the family; since then no one had had the energy to replace it.

"It was too much trouble," said the Taliaferros, who pronounced their name "Tollyver."

Jo's father did make a half-hearted effort; he wandered North from his home in Alabama, and ran away with old Snyder B. Simes's daughter and only child. Snyder B. Simes, lumber-merchant, was a Maine man who had made his pile himself and meant to keep it; he burned his daughter's letters unopened, and made a new will.

"If my money 's to be spent in riotous living, I mean to spend it myself," he said, buttoning up his pockets.

Mrs. Taliaferro burst into tears when she first saw her new Southern home; then she got up and put on an apron and began to clean the house; this she continued to do until the day of her death. She never learned to adjust herself to her surroundings, nor that it is sometimes a good woman's duty to ignore dirt. She washed and scrubbed and cleaned, and was finally swept out of this world on a sea of soap-suds,—another martyr to the great god of cleanliness.

She left one little boy behind her, named Jo, to the care, or, more properly speaking, to the neglect of his father.

"Do you see that man?" said the superintendent of the great Brookville Glass Works, which Northern capital had lately planted in Brookville County, Alabama—"do you see that man?" He was pointing out Jo's father. "Well, you will never see him doing any more than he is now; nobody ever saw him work. He eats, drinks, clothes himself, has a roof over his head, and not a cent in his pocket. Now, how does he do it? And there are a dozen like him about here. I tell you, the mysteries of Paris are nothing to the mysteries of Brookville."

And as we can never permit our minds to dwell on a subject without hearing of it again within twenty-four hours, that same day the superintendent received a letter from Jo.

The spelling was dubious and the handwriting shaky; but there was nothing dubious or shaky in the spirit of the composition.

MISTER SUPERINTENDANT,—I wud like a Plac in yor employ.

JO TOLLY.

P. S. Taliaferro is to long and quar.

The superintendent laughed as he tossed this evident result of anxious labour in the scrap-basket. The next week he received a fac-simile of that letter, minus the postscript, to which he accorded a similar treatment; but when he saw those same straggling characters on an envelope in his mail the third week, he opened it with an amused curiosity.

MISTER SUPERINTENDANT, — I wrot you 2 Letters and hav no ansar. I wod like to be in yor employ, but I kant wait; I mus git a job. Pleas, sir, ansar and oblig. JO TOLLY.

The superintendent's hand with the paper in it hovered over the scrap-basket; then he drew it back. At his call a weak-kneed young man came in from the outer office.

"Have you room for another boy out there?" the superintendent asked. "You have. Well, then, write to this applicant and tell him he may come on trial."

For the first few weeks Jo Tolly was like a new-born puppy out in the world with its eyes shut.

"You must look about you, Tolly," said the head clerk. "Now, I started out with no money, no education, no backing, and here I am, all by keeping my eyes peeled."

The clerk with the weak knees struck in: "Look at me," he said. "I 've been a sober, honest, industrious, God-fearing man for fifteen years, and not a cent to show for it."

Jo turned his long, ruddy face and big, innocent blue eyes from one to the other, and said nothing. He rarely talked, and when he did, it was with a deliberate slowness which barely escaped a drawl. But he pondered all that he heard in his heart, apparently; for gradually his puppydom fell from him, and he became a satisfactory fixture in the office.

The Brookville Glass Works were a close corporation. They had bought up two thousand acres about the site selected for their works. Their labourers dwelt in their cottages built on their land; they bought from the company store, and lived under laws of their directors' making.

But there was a Naboth's vineyard in the centre of the settlement. The trouble was that old Colonel Jay respected his ancestors, and refused to listen to any proposition regarding their sale,— for the "vineyard" was a family burying-ground this time. The superintendent vainly represented to him that the bones should be carefully removed.

"They are earth to earth by this time, sir," said Colonel Jay, with stateliness. "When I sell that ground, sir, I sell them; so we will not mention it again, if you please, sir."

After that the superintendent, who suspected a pistol in every Alabama pocket, did not care to open the subject again.

"Ain't you ever goin' to sell, Colonel Jay?" asked Jo.

He had paddled across the creek which separated the Glass Works from the old man's house, and was sitting on his porch with him in the twilight.

"No, sir; nor I ain't ever going to accommodate again, neither. I told those Dixies they might bury their little babby there, and what did they do? Laid it right on great-grandaunt 'Liza. I went and told them they 'd got to take that babby off. But it warn't pleasant. I won't accommodate again."

"And you ain't ever goin' to sell, Colonel Jay?"

"Look here, Jo," said the colonel, testily, "how old are you? Eighteen years. Well, I guess you remember me as soon as you remember anything. Did you ever know me to change my mind? That ground ain't ever to be disturbed!" he added with finality.

Jo turned his full blue eyes on the colonel: "How about when you die, Colonel Jay?" he asked in his most deliberate speech.

The colonel was staggered and showed it.

"If I were you," Jo went on, now looking over the water, "I'd fix that while I was able. There's a whole acre there, and there ain't but one end of it in graves. I'd sell it all under a deed that would make the man who bought it keep the grave end nice and clean, and the grass cut — and perhaps flowers."

Colonel Jay rose from his chair. "Boy," he cried, "you're right! Why did n't I think of that?" Then his face fell suddenly. "But who'd be fool enough to buy?"

"I would," answered Jo, stolidly; "and if I don't pay you a hundred dollars for it in a year's time, you can take the ground back and all the improvements on it."

What the improvements meant, the whole Works soon knew. "Jo Tolly's store" was the talk of the place. It was little more than a shanty; but the labourers soon learned that the shanty had goods of better quality and lower price on its shelves than the Company's handsome store-house had on theirs.

"It ain't very pretty outside, but I tried to have it good in," said Jo, modestly, looking at the well-stocked walls. "I spent all my money there."

The money referred to was a small sum which he had obtained by auctioning off the worn-out roof which covered him, and the bit of land on which it stood; the rest of the tract had been sold almost to the very door-step long before. There had been no one to interfere in his reinvestment, his father having performed the first graceful act in his worthless life by stepping out of it at this opportune time.

"Don't spend all your money in shoestrings and rock-candy, Tolly," the superintendent had said. "Put it in the bank, and try to keep adding to your bank-book. That 's the way."

"Yes, sir," said Jo, submissively; but at the same time it was not his way, nor did he follow it.

At first the Tolly store was only open at night, and Jo waited on the customers after hours; but as the business grew, a small boy kept store by day and was assistant to the proprieter at night.

"I should n't think you 'd dare, Jo; I should n't, indeed," said the weak-kneed clerk, who came to inspect his enterprise by stealth and after nightfall. "Why, I would n't even like the chief to see me come in here; and how can you sleep right next to those graves?"

"I like them," said Jo, showing the first sign of interest; "I 'm getting real fond of them. I like Aunt 'Liza, and I feel like I knew Aunt Jane.

"'Dear friends, repent; no more delay,
For death will come, to take no nay.
Be always ready, night and day;
I suddenly was snatched away.'

I feel just like she was saying it to me every time I read it."

The head clerk — he of the "peeled eyes" — also paid Jo a visit; but he came in by broad daylight, and examined everything. He laughed a good deal, and looked at Jo's placid face curiously.

"You 're bucking against a big concern, boy," he said. "I tell you, you 'll have to work like an ox and kick like a steer."

Jo, smiling his usual rather stupid, slow smile, listened to each one, and said nothing.

As yet the superintendent had said nothing either, but that came. One day, as Jo was passing through his office, he stopped him. "Tolly," he said carelessly, "how much do you hold your land at?"

"What do you think it 's worth, sir?" inquired Jo, respectfully.

"Not much."

"I 've got my store built and paid for out of it," Jo went on, as though calculating aloud; "I 've paid for my land; the business is growing, and —"

"You take a week to think it over in," said the superintendent, hastily.

On that day week Jo entered the superintendent's office, and stood before his desk.

"Well, Tolly," said the superintendent, "what is it?"

"It 's ten thousand dollars," said Jo.

When the superintendent had a little recovered he knew that he was a very angry man, and at the same time that it behooved him to walk carefully.

"The directors could n't consider such a price," he said; "it would n't be worth it to them."

"No, sir," said Jo, meekly; "I know it ain't worth much to anybody but me."

Then it was that the superintendent gave Jo very clearly to understand that he considered him infringing on the rights of the company in whose service he was.

The boy looked so puzzled that he melted somewhat. "You don't understand me."

"No, sir," said Jo; "I thought I owned the land."

"So you do," said the superintendent, reassuringly, feeling now on sure ground; "but not for all purposes."

"I thought I could put a saloon on it if I wanted to," said Jo, in a depressed voice.

The superintendent's hair almost stood on end; a grog-shop in the midst of his Works! He could hardly conceal his dismay.

"Tolly," he said sternly, "you must choose between the office and your shop; no man can serve two masters."

"Yes, sir; you are very kind, sir," said Jo, looking gratefully at him. "I was thinking my clerk was n't doing as well as he might if I had my eye more on him."

"And I assure you, gentlemen," said the superintendent, reporting to the Board of Directors at their next meeting, "when that boy left my office I did not know whether it was as a fool, or as having made a fool of me."

"Call the lad in," suggested one of the directors. "Let us see if we can make anything of him."

Jo came in at once on being summoned; he did not even tarry to take off the apron which he wore in his shop, or to brush the flour from his coat. These adjuncts helped to heighten the ruddy innocence of his appearance as he entered. He faced the curious eyes of the waiting Board with a disarming guilelessness.

"Did you want me, sir," he asked of the superintendent, and the slow motion of his lips was almost foolish.

But had those lips only been formed to say "ten thousand" they could not have repeated it more persistently when the question of barter was opened. His slow-moving blue eyes looked with open, childish appeal into the assembled faces.

"I do think it 's worth that to me, sir, don't you?"

he asked of the most urgent speaker; and that gentleman suddenly collapsed.

There was one director who took no part in the controversy; he sat in his chair rubbing his hands together and watching the scene from his keen, deep-set eyes. Every now and then his spare frame was shaken with silent laughter. As the door closed on Jo's retreating figure, he gave way to spasms of alternate laughter and coughing.

"Oh, Lord, Lord!" he chuckled, wiping his eyes, "to have that fool-look on the outside of his head and all that horse-sense on the inside!"

"Then, sir, you think him playing a game, do you?" asked the superintendent.

"Playing? He's played it! Hasn't he caught us in just the trap he started out to?" The old man went off in another paroxysm of laughter. "What did you say the lad's name was," he gasped as he recovered.

"Jo Tolly," answered the disgusted superintendent, "or, rather, that's what he calls himself; his real name is T-a-l-i-a-f-e-r-r-o."

"Taliaferro,—Joseph Taliaferro. What was his father's name?"

"Joseph, also, I believe."

"It's him! As sure as my name's Snyder B. Simes, it's him!" cried the old man, rising to his feet, excitedly. "Where's he gone? Where's he gone?"

He rushed from the room, his thin legs wavering under him, followed by the bewildered superintendent. When they returned, Jo Tolly, divested of the flour and apron now, was with them.

"Gentlemen," said Mr. Snyder B. Simes, "allow me to present my grandson to you, formerly of the firm of 'Jo Tolly,' now full-pledged partner of the lumber firm of 'Snyder B. Simes & Grandson.' The Tolly store is *closed*, gentlemen. We — that is, my partner has decided that it is more advantageous for our present business to be on agreeable terms with this Brookville Glass Works Company."

Here Mr. Simes, shaking with laughter, broke down again.

"Oh, boys, ain't he a chip of the old block?" he cried. "What will you have, gentlemen? It 's the firm's treat."

THE GENTLEMAN-IN-PLUSH.

THE GENTLEMAN-IN-PLUSH.

"What is good for a bootless bene?

"Whence can comfort spring,
When prayer is of no avail?"

WORDSWORTH.

WASSISETTI LAKE, one of Nature's tearful dimples, lies in the midst of the Wassisetti Hills in Canada. It is fed by unobtrusive springs and streams; and although not long or wide, its depth is in places unfathomable.

Among its many coves is one where the hills run almost sheerly down on all three sides, cutting off the winds, and throwing gloomy shadows on the quiet water. A tiny stream trickles down the slope, and its tinkle as it drops into the lake is the only sound which breaks the oppressive stillness. In winter, when the cold has frozen the stream into silence and hushed that indefinable soft murmur of summer growth which some have ears to hear, this spot seems unbearably desolate.

Yet on a cold Christmas afternoon, a man's figure might have been seen standing on the small platform of land formed by a bend of the hill before it dropped into the lake. Nor was he without personal surroundings.

There was a tiny hut on the platform, built of rudest materials, but carefully constructed. The foundations were of stone, evidently taken from the hillside, for their former companions still lay there; the walls were of logs daubed with mud.

The man was standing looking up into the branches of a tall spruce-tree, on which a cluster of unusually large and beautiful cones was growing. He was dressed in a complete suit of brown corduroy, and as he stood with his head thrown back his face was an interesting study. His hair was quite white, while the eyebrows and closely clipped mustache and pointed beard were black. There were deep lines scored in his forehead, and sweeping lines ran also from the sensitive nostrils toward the corners of the lips. But the eyes were his most striking feature; in colour they were a peculiar red-brown, and in expression strangely introspective, or what is better known as deep.

When the man began climbing the tree, which he presently did, his motions were more stiff than agile. The boughs were crusted with ice, yet he climbed into them with a carelessness which amounted to recklessness. As his hand touched the cones, he started, and almost fell from his perch.

A queer little voice had broken the stillness. "He 's d-dressed all in plush," it said whisperingly.

Two little children, a boy and a girl, stood hand in hand under the tree gazing up at the climber, who looked at them and laughed.

"Catch," he said, as he plucked the cones and flung them down on their heads.

When he reached the ground himself, he walked up to the children and held out his arm.

"Would you like to feel the plush?" he asked.

It was evident that even to these childish minds his appearance was unusual. The little girl, who was the elder by several years, drew back; but the boy dragged his hand from hers, and laid it on the corduroy sleeve.

"It 's s-soft," he said, looking up into the man's face, and answering his smile.

It was the same queer little voice that had spoken before. There was a slight hesitation in his speech and in the child's manner; he was a fragile-looking little fellow. The stranger noted the delicacy of his hands as they lay on his sleeve, blue with the cold; he took them in his, and rubbed them gently.

"Where are your gloves?" he asked; for in every other respect the boy was carefully protected.

"Nurse has them. We r-runned away."

The smiling face changed suddenly. "Where do you live?"

"In the big house on the hill. We 've c-comed home."

"And what is your name?"

"Urwick Manly — and s-she 's Gladys."

The man gazed abstractedly out over the frozen lake, and, with the quick perception of childhood, the boy knew that his presence was forgotten. He moved his little hands, which yet lay in the stranger's, uneasily, and thus roused, the man looked down kindly, but still evidently with his thoughts elsewhere.

"Run home, now, both of you, or nurse will be anxious," he said. "You may take the cones with you."

The children trudged away obediently by a rough bridle-path which ran about the hills, but so long as they were in sight the boy kept turning back, crying: "Good-by, Gentleman-in-Plush, good-by!"

The Gentleman-in-Plush stood before the door of his hut with his hand on the latch. He looked at the poor dwelling, and behind it at the bare branches of the trees on the hill, a network against the gray sky; he looked at the bleak cove in its ice setting and magnificent dreariness.

"Not even this left!" he said aloud, and passed in.

Mr. Manly, the owner of the house on the hill, was a tall, fine-looking Canadian who had married an English wife, and they had just returned from a visit of nearly a year at her father's home. He had laughed so heartily at the account of a tramp in plush, that the day after Christmas, Urwick insisted on guiding him to the hut in the cove, that he might see with his own eyes.

"I can stand anything but tramps," said Mr. Manly, "and I expect to find one housed under every bush, not all of them 'gentlemen-in-plush,' either—eh, Urwick?"

Urwick, riding on his little pony by his father's side, looked hurt and said nothing. His father, with all his kindness, did not quite understand him, and was rather fond of teasing him.

Leaving the beaten road they struck off into a bridle-path, which led up and down hills which might have been dangerous riding had the Canadian horses been any less rough-shod or surefooted.

"There 's his house," said Urwick, when they reached the cove.

Mr. Manly rode up to the hut and examined the structure.

"The coolness of the beggar!" he said, as he rapped on the door with the handle of his riding-stock. "It 's pretty well built, though."

Had he been on his own feet instead of on his horse's back, Mr. Manly would have started back at the appearance of the man who almost immediately opened the door.

"That 's the G-Gentleman-in-Plush, Papa," Urwick whispered.

"It is Mr. Manly, I suppose. You will pardon me for not inviting you into your own house," said the stranger, quietly. His voice was low, and his enunciation peculiarly cultivated.

"What are you doing here?" asked Mr. Manly.

The question was so evidently the result of an extreme surprise, and not roughness, that the stranger smiled as he answered,—

"Have your outbuildings never been infested by tramps before?"

"By tramps? Yes—"

"That is the class of society to which I belong. I have been here for six months; longer than I have rested anywhere in as many years."

Mr. Manly looked about him and shivered at the aspect. "With the whole farm to choose from, why, in Heaven's name, did you pitch on this spot?" he asked.

"Tramps have fancies as well as other men."

"Why attempt that rôle?" said Mr. Manly, a little impatiently.

"I should think you might consider that I had acted it consistently. I have used your land as a home, your timber for building, your fire-wood for warmth, and am now prepared to be driven out as an ordinary intruder."

"What you speak of has no value," returned Mr. Manly, quickly. He was as uncomfortable as if he had been the one caught trespassing. "There is no question of driving you out. You are welcome to stay here as long as you want,—which would not be long if I were in your place." He again glanced around the dreary amphitheatre of skeleton trees and ice.

The man's eyes followed his. "Yet I have known some peaceful hours here," he said, "and I am grateful to you for the permission."

Mr. Manly paused before he spoke again. "As yet, The Gentleman-in-Plush is the only name you have," he said.

They both looked at Urwick, who had sat quietly on his pony listening. The stranger smiled.

"As well that as another," he replied at last; "will Dennis Plush satisfy you, Mr. Manly?"

"As you will," answered Mr. Manly, somewhat stiffly. "Good-morning. Come, Urwick."

But Urwick stopped to shake hands in farewell. "Good-by, G-Gentleman-in-Plush," he said, in his odd little voice. "I will come again to visit you some day, — p-perhaps to-morrow."

"Well, Urwick," said Mr. Manly, as his son joined him, "you were only half wrong, after all, my boy. Your tramp was not dressed in plush; but, stranger still, he is a gentleman, and I was the embarrassed one, not he."

Not only on the morrow, but on many successive days, did Urwick visit the hut in the cove. The two children, for Gladys often accompanied him, were the only human beings who ever entered its walls.

When it became necessary to replenish his larder, the Gentleman-in-Plush, as the children still called him, would walk over to the neighbouring village and make his purchases, calling at the post-office for a periodic letter which came addressed to "A. B. C.;" and then, having spoken no unnecessary word, he would return to his hut.

Mr. Manly formed the habit of riding down the hill

once or twice a week with a pocketful of English papers and periodicals, which he found were the only small comforts not refused with steady decision. He would sit on the horse's back at the hut door chatting with the recluse, but he was never invited to enter.

"Dennis Plush is evidently a cultivated gentleman with a tile loose somewhere," said Mr. Manly. "What do you and your mysterious friend find to talk about, Urwick?"

"He 's trying to teach me n-not to stammer, and s-some other little things," the boy answered.

Later Mr. Manly found out what the other little things were. As a surprise on his birthday, Urwick proudly recited to him an ode of Horace and some lines of Homer.

"The Gentleman-in-Plush taught me," he said.

There had been trouble in the Manly household over Urwick's education; for even his father recognized that he was unfit for boarding-school.

It was an unexpected solution, and one which was gratefully accepted, when the Gentleman-in-Plush offered to undertake the boy's education. He taught him in the hut through the rest of the winter, and when summer came gave him lessons in woodcraft and botany, thus, by gentle degrees, interesting the delicate boy in outdoor pursuits. He cured him of his inborn shrinking from the lake by which he lived; and the two spent days in exploring its jagged shore, thrusting the nose of their canoe in every inlet and secluded nook. He taught him also to watch the habits of the small wild animals in the wood; for there seemed a strange familiarity and affinity between these shy dumb creatures and the man who dwelt among them from month to month with only a little child as companion.

So the seasons slipped by, one after the other. Gladys was but eight years old when the Gentleman-in-Plush was first discovered in his hut, and when her fourteenth birthday came he was still there. On the afternoon of that day Mrs. Manly sought her husband with a troubled look on her fair, motherly face.

"I want to speak to you," she said; "something so strange has happened."

She opened her hand, on the palm of which lay a ring, with its old-fashioned setting holding a pink pearl, surrounded by diamonds.

"The Gentleman-in-Plush gave it to Gladys," she said gravely.

Mr. Manly took the ring and examined it. "It looks like an heirloom, and it may be. It is no more mysterious than the man has always been; there is something very odd about the whole affair, — nothing worse than eccentricity, though. There is no reason that Gladys should not keep his gift."

But Mrs. Manly still looked troubled. "This is the least strange part of it. He gave Gladys the ring, telling her that she was a young lady now, and might wear it. At the same time he sent me a message, which Gladys was crying too much to deliver clearly; but the child understood from it that she was not to go to the hut after this."

Mr. Manly was indignant. "Nonsense! Why not? She is a mere baby. Tell Gladys she sha'n't be made to cry on her birthday. I will go to the cove myself and see Plush about it."

The door of the hut was opened before Mr. Manly could knock. "I heard your horse's feet," said the Gentleman-in-Plush.

Mr. Manly plunged at once into the matter on his mind. "I came to see you about Gladys, Plush. What nonsense have you been talking to the child?"

"I supposed that was what you had come for. Will you walk into the hut, Mr. Manly?" The invitation was as quietly given as if it had not been delayed for six years.

Mr. Manly, interested and surprised, tied his horse, and entered, looking around him not without a stirring of curiosity.

One end of the small room was neatly curtained off — he judged to conceal a bed, as none was visible elsewhere. The walls on the inside, as on the out, were of rough tree-trunks, with the bark still on them. A rudely made table, two chairs, and a stool were in one corner, and a stove, with cooking utensils hanging behind it, in another.

The only difference between this interior and that of an ordinary woodman's hut, lay in its exquisite cleanliness and in the presence of a book-shelf standing against the wall. This shelf of books must have been conspicuous in a well-furnished room, but in the rude setting of the hut the crimson and purple and gold and blue of the rich bindings glowed like the jewel in a toad's head.

Mr. Manly hardly repressed an exclamation. His companion seemed unconscious of his surprise. He motioned him toward a chair; and then — for the shadows were falling — he drew the curtains over the windows, and lighting a candle, set it on the table. There was a repressed agitation in his silence, and Mr. Manly, silent also, waited with a strange interest, which became intense when his host brought out a portfolio from behind the screen and laid it on the table by the candle. As the light fell on it, Mr. Manly saw that the edges and clasps were of silver, and that a coat-of-arms had evidently been torn from the back, for the uncertain impress of a shield and crest and mantle were still visible on the leather.

"Will you read this?" said the Gentleman-in-Plush.

He drew a letter from its envelope and handed it to Mr. Manly, who noticed that his hand trembled and that his form seemed shrunken. He looked to him suddenly a hundred years old.

If the reader expected to gain much knowledge from the letter, he was mistaken. It was signed with a woman's name—"Harriet Eleanore Grey"—and was a generalization of scathing denunciations. It cut off forever the soul to whom it was addressed from the writer, from those in whose name she wrote, even it seemed from all human kind and Heaven's mercy itself.

Mr. Manly laid the letter down with a gesture of horror; words of indignation were on his lips, when his companion's passionless voice stopped them.

"That letter was written by my mother's sister, the gentlest woman in all England."

As the letter was replaced in the envelope, Mr. Manly involuntarily glanced at the superscription. A part of it was torn away, but he read:

To the Honourable Dennis Fl——
Glen——
England.

And he sat like a man in a dream. He was roused by something being laid on the table before him; it was the portrait of a woman, painted on ivory and framed in gold. The face was beautiful, although more proud than strong.

"That is my wife," said the same mechanical voice.

"Is she living?" Mr. Manly could not repress the question.

"No; I killed her as surely as by poison or steel. There are other ways—and—more cruel." He rose and closed the portfolio.

Mr. Manly, feeling himself dismissed, rose also, but not silently; his pity rose higher than his companion's reserve.

"Plush," he said, "or whatever you please to call yourself, I don't know in what way you have sinned against your family and society, but I do know that hiding is no reparation. Go back to your people, and live it down among them."

The hands of the man thus urged closed convulsively over the back of the chair by which he stood; for a moment Mr. Manly thought that he clung to it for support. His face was gray, and his lips were white; twice he tried vainly to speak.

"I have two sons, and, did I ever pray, I should pray God that they may never know more of me than they do now."

His tones were without pulse or feeling; he was as passionless as a dead man.

It was Mr. Manly's voice that sounded human, and that broke when he answered: "God send you a prayer, and a better one!"

As he turned away, the exile followed him, and laid his hand on his arm, for the first time speaking and acting entirely as an equal; yet his words were entreatingly humble.

"You will let me see the boy sometimes, Manly?"

Mr. Manly nearly broke down again when, excitedly

striding up and down his wife's room, he told her of the interview.

"It was like a lost soul in hell praying for a drop of water," he said. "Think of a man of birth and position falling to this! You must lend him the boy, Mabel, whenever you can spare him."

"And Gladys?" asked Mrs. Manly.

Mr. Manly ceased his walk, and stood looking thoughtfully out of the window toward the cove. His wife repeated her question, —

"Shall I send Gladys, too, dear?"

"I don't believe he would permit it," said her husband, evasively; and then she knew what he wished her to do.

Whether he imagined it, or whether that unsealing of the long-closed springs opened a torrent of haunting thought which wore on the body of the Gentleman-in-Plush, Mr. Manly did not know; but to his eyes he seemed changed and aged after that day.

There was no further reference made by either to their strange interview, and the only alteration it caused was in Urwick's more constant presence at the hut, and Gladys's absence.

A few weeks later it happened that Mr. Manly dined at the same house with his bishop, in a neighbouring town.

"I had thought I should meet you here, Manly," said his lordship, "and I have brought a letter with me about which I wish to ask your help. It is from a lady in England; she says that she has reason to think that her sister's son — not a young man, by her description — is in Canada, and in your county."

"Can you let me see the letter?" said Mr. Manly, with quick interest.

Before he opened it, he knew that the name signed would be "Harriet Eleanore Grey."

The letter requested that the bishop would notify the writer if he found the man still living, as in the event of his death the question of a title was involved.

"No other news of him can now hold anything but pain for his family," the letter ended.

Mr. Manly returned it with a sigh of disappointment.

"It is like seeking a needle in a haystack, I fear," said the bishop.

"No," answered Mr. Manly; "this world seems but little larger than an apple sometimes. I do know the man, and know him too well to betray him; but I will undertake to notify you should anything happen to him, which I should wish a time far off, were he any less unhappy than I think he is."

"They are a wicked, hard, cruel people," said Mrs. Manly, when she heard the story.

But her husband stirred his library fire reflectively, before he answered: "I don't know; remorse is not repentance. The whole thing is mysterious, and I have no judgment in the matter."

The winter had set in bitterly cold that year; the lake froze over so hard and deep that a team of oxen was driven from one end of it to the other in safety. There came some days when it was impossible for Urwick to go to the hut through the snow and ice. One morning, after having been weather-bound in this way for some time, he came home with a frightened expression on his face.

"My Gentleman-in-Plush is very ill," he said in an awe-struck voice; "will you go to him, Papa? He can't get out of bed."

Mr. Manly went, but returned to his house almost immediately to order that the doctor should be sent for, and that warm bedding and stimulants should be carried to the hut.

"I am afraid Plush is a very ill man," he said; "it looks like pneumonia, and he has exposed himself recklessly."

When the doctor came his opinion bore out this theory. The Gentleman-in-Plush was very ill. But toward evening Mr. Manly came home with a better report; he had left the physician and a servant in charge.

"I shall go down later and spend the night," he said. "There seems no present danger."

Urwick, who had been wandering miserably about the house all day, asking persistently, "Is my Gentleman-in-Plush dying?" went to bed comforted.

They thought him fast asleep when a hurried summons came from the hut; there had been a sudden sinking of the patient's vital forces, and the worst might be feared.

"Let me go with you," entreated Mrs. Manly; "he can hardly resent it now, and he has been so good to our boy."

Mr. Manly assented; but when, cloaked for her walk, Mrs. Manly joined him in the hall, she was looking more troubled and distressed than before.

"You must go to Urwick; I can do nothing with him. He heard us talking, and insists on going with us. I thought him half asleep when he came stumbling into my room. I have never seen him like this before."

"Do you go down with the servant," her husband answered; "I will follow you."

He found Urwick sitting on the floor of his room in his nightgown. He was sobbing bitterly as he struggled with his shoes and stockings.

"I w-will go; I promised," he cried when he saw his father.

The stammer which his friend had taught him to control came back in his excitement. He stood up and stamped his small foot and clenched his hands.

His father lifted him in his great arms and held him firmly; he hardly recognized the gentle little fellow in this frantic child who struggled and almost struck him.

"I will go,—I w-will. I promised the G-Gentleman-in-Plush,—I promised."

"What did you promise, Urwick? Stop struggling, my boy, and speak slowly."

The steady strength of his father's clasp and voice had their influence.

"I promised; l-long ago I promised. I promised I would come to him wherever I was if he were dying, and I heard my mother say he was dying now."

"I hope not; but if you have made a promise you must run no risk of breaking it. And you must stop crying, you know, before you can go. Can you dress yourself?"

But though Urwick asserted that he could, his father stayed by him, steadying the quivering nerves by word and touch, unconsciously laying in those moments the foundations of an understanding between himself and that most delicate and difficult of all created things, a sensitive child's heart.

When, half an hour later, Mrs. Manly opened the door of the hut, and her husband entered, covered with the fine flecks of the falling snow, he had on his back what she at first thought was a bundle of shawls; but when he set it down before her, she discovered that Urwick was the core of the roll.

"Did you think it wise to bring him?" she asked, dismayed.

"It was because I promised, Mamma," said the child, eagerly. And Mrs. Manly, who rarely questioned her husband's decisions, said no more.

The screen had been taken down, and the Gentleman-in-Plush lay on his bed with his eyes closed. The physician was preparing to leave.

"It is stupor," he said; "he will not rouse from it, I think; but should he do so there is nothing to do or say that Mrs. Manly is not better fitted for than I."

Urwick crept quietly to a chair at the head of the bed, and the husband and wife talked in whispers at the side. There seemed little to do but wait.

Suddenly the sick man moved, and opened his eyes. "Am I dying?" he asked briefly.

"I trust not, oh, I trust not,— not if we can keep you with us," said Mrs. Manly.

He looked full into her kind face with his strange, deep eyes.

"Thank you," he said gently, then turned from her to her husband, and spoke with wonderful strength of voice; "You have been kind, Manly, and I am going to ask for six feet more from you. Will you let me stay here in the hut?"

"I want you to stay in it a live man," said Mr. Manly. "Take this, Plush."

But the Gentleman-in-Plush pushed the stimulant away.

"I have written the boy's name in the books," he went on; "and, Manly, you remember a portfolio I once showed you? Bury it with me. That is all." He turned wearily away.

"Have you nothing more to say?" asked Mr. Manly.

"Nothing."

"Think again. Is there no message I can send to your family?"

An expression of ineffable pain passed over the drawn face; the words dropped with difficulty from the white lips.

"Nothing—I have no kindred, no country, no hope—nothing."

His eyes closed, and they would have thought the stupor had returned, except that his lips kept forming the words: "Nothing—nothing."

"Speak to him, Mabel. For God's sake, speak to him!" whispered Mr. Manly, in a choked voice; and his wife, with the tears raining down her face, knelt by the bedside and began a prayer.

The hand on the coverlid was raised with an imperious gesture, and Mrs. Manly's voice faltered and died away.

Presently, when she bent over him again, he opened his eyes and looked up into her face.

"Rosalie," he said wanderingly, "Rosalie, can it be you?"

"He is wandering!" Mrs. Manly exclaimed pitifully. "It is his wife's name, perhaps."

"Rosalie," went on the wandering voice, "why, they told me you were dead—that you died when—"

"Urwick, what are you about?" said Mr. Manly, sternly.

The child had crept upon the other side of the bed, and his hand was on his friend's lips.

He wound his arm about the neck of the Gentleman-in-Plush, and clasped him closely when his father tried to lift him.

"I promised — I promised," he cried again.

Mrs. Manly laid her hand on her husband's arm, and drew him away.

"Don't you see?" she said through her tears. "He has wished to die as he lived. We must let them be."

And Mr. Manly, looking wonderingly at the strange sight, sat silently awaiting the end.

The night wore on, but still the weary childish body and the ready little hand kept guard; at each murmur the wandering lips were sealed. The mother's heart yearned over the eyes heavy with sleep, and the cheeks pale with the vigil.

But she, too, sat silent until the dying man opened his eyes once more, and looked with loving recognition into the anxious child's face on the pillow by him.

With an expression which was in itself a caress, he lifted the faithful little hand from his lips and held it between his own.

"He knows me, Mamma! He will get well!" cried the boy, eagerly.

And at that moment, with a short, sighing breath, holding fast by the frail anchor of a child's hand, the weary soul of the Gentleman-in-Plush passed away from the judgments of this world.

They buried him in the hut, as he had wished, and

his secret with him. As there came only a formal acknowledgment from England in response to the bishop's announcement of his death, Mr. Manly placed the slab which now lies over his grave. It bears no name,—only a date and a line of inscription,—

"*After life's fitful fever, he sleeps well.*"

A TEA-LEAF.

A Tea-Leaf.

A PSYCHOLOGICAL STUDY IN ONE ACT.

Dramatis Personæ: Mr. Robert May; Miss Littell.

Time: *Miss* Littell's *reception afternoon, half-past five o'clock.*

Curtain rises on a nineteenth-century drawing-room, and discovers Mr. May *sitting on a long, low bench which runs in front of a three-cornered fireplace. He sits with his back to the fire, and faces Miss* Littell, *who is engrossed in pouring fragrant tea into Russian tea-glasses. A dainty triangular tea-table stands at her left hand, and a hissing kettle of water hangs from a wrought-iron crane over the hot coals. Some confusion in the room and the languor of Miss* Littell's *manner betoken departed guests.*

Miss Littell (*poising a lump of sugar in the sugar-tongs*). You take one lump of sugar, do you not, and lemon?

Mr. May. No, not lemon; a drop of cream, please.

Miss Littell (*with rising inflection*). Cream!

Mr May. Well, no; not when you put it in that way. Don't look horrified, but give me the lemon.

Miss Littell. Not at all. If you want a flavourless dilution, you shall have it.

(*She stretches out her hand toward the cream, but Mr.* May *ends the controversy by seizing the pitcher and placing it out of her reach. He helps himself to lemon with an air of mock misery.*)

Mr. MAY. Have all your callers been so successfully managed?

Miss LITTELL (*laughing and sipping her tea*). No; no one represented much material for management or amusement. Each was deplorably like the other, and very correct in type. One little *débutante* was rather delicious. She told me that she and her brother had been talking about me, and under pressure it came out that they were wondering why I did not marry. "Joe told me he knew you had had lots of chances," she said. I thought that was very kind of Joe, don't you?

Mr. MAY. Very.

Miss LITTELL. I asked her if Joe suggested that I might prefer living with two devoted brothers to marrying one husband. "Oh, no," she said, opening her eyes; "do you really feel that way? How funny!" Was n't that charming?

Mr. MAY (*with a perfectly mirthless face*). Ha-ha!

(*Miss* LITTELL *starts and looks at him sharply. Mr.* MAY *is silent. He sits on the bench, and stares moodily over his shoulder into the fire.*)

Miss LITTELL (*nervously*). The room seems gloomy; I must ring for lights.

(*As she puts out her hand toward the bell, Mr.* MAY *suddenly catches it in both of his.*)

Mr. MAY. Pray do not. I have something to say to you, and even the firelight seems too much.

(*He rises to his feet, knocking over the fire-irons in his confusion. As he stoops to pick them up Miss* LITTELL *falls back in her chair, staring at him in dismay.*)

Miss LITTELL (*aside*). Is Robert, my old friend Robert, going to do this thing? Is our friendship to be wrecked upon the old, keel-worn rock? Never. I will stop him before he begins.

(*She tries to speak, but her tongue cleaves to the roof of her mouth.*)

Mr. MAY. You must have guessed — you certainly know —

Miss LITTELL (*wildly*). No, no; I don't know anything, — I don't want to know.

Mr. MAY (*gloomily turning away*). That won't alter the fact. I have always known that you disliked Mary; but you must have suspected our engagement.

Miss LITTELL (*aside and faintly*). What did I say! (*The danger just brushed renders her voice tremulous as she speaks aloud.*) This has been a great shock to me, Robert, but you know that I wish you every hap —

Mr. MAY. Stop, for Heaven's sake! (*He paces the floor in agitation. Suddenly he pauses in front of* Miss LITTELL, *and speaks abruptly.*) Do you consider me a man devoid of any honourable instincts?

Miss LITTELL (*with emphasis*). I know you to be upright and true-hearted; you are a man of absolute honour. But you thoroughly bewilder me, Robert; won't you sit down and tell me what you mean?

(Mr. MAY *sits down on the low bench again, and looks up at her.*)

Mr. MAY. What would you say if I should tell you that I am desperately, passionately in love with two women to-night?

Miss LITTELL (*promptly*). I should say that I trusted I was not one of them.

Mr. MAY. I am not laughing. You must listen seriously. I am very unhappy.

Miss LITTELL. I should think you might be. Most

people can get all the misery they want out of one love affair at a time. Mary is one of the girls, of course; and who is the other? (*After a silence Miss* LITTELL *says slowly.*) Not Elizabeth, surely! You would not have dared to drag her into folly of this sort.

Mr. MAY. There 's no height of daring or depth of folly which I have not tried.

Miss LITTELL (*still incredulous*). What are you going to do about it? As you are engaged to Mary, I gather that she is the one you mean to marry.

Mr. MAY. Never while I live.

Miss LITTELL. Then, if you don't mean to marry her, would you mind telling me why you are engaged to her?

Mr. MAY (*briefly*). Because I love her.

Miss LITTELL (*with mild sarcasm*). I am afraid I am very stupid, Robert; but, really, I cannot understand. Is it that you love Mary and won't marry her, and will marry Elizabeth and don't love her? It is all very confusing.

Mr. MAY (*laughing miserably*). Don't jeer at me. I am fallen low enough, I assure you.

Miss LITTELL. Have you been making love to both girls, Robert? Don't tell me that.

Mr. MAY. No, no; I loved Elizabeth with all my heart and soul, long before I ever saw Mary. I never told her so, for I thought it useless; and Mary —

Miss LITTELL. Mary assured you that it was — I understand.

Mr. MAY. It was never done directly. I did not dream that she suspected my feeling for Elizabeth. Among a hundred other things, she repeated one remark of Elizabeth's which was simple enough in itself, but certainly conclusive.

Miss LITTELL. Would you mind telling me what Mary repeated?

Mr. MAY (*with embarrassment*). It sounds silly in the repetition, and yet it finally convinced me.

Miss LITTELL (*gently persistent*). Can't you tell me what it was?

Mr. MAY (*with an effort*). Oh, yes. She said no power could induce her to marry a man with big ears.

Miss LITTELL (*vainly struggling against her laughter*). Oh, Robert, Robert! I did not know your vanity was as great as your ears.

Mr. MAY (*earnestly*). It was not a question of vanity. I thought no woman could speak in that manner of the man she cared for.

Miss LITTELL. Then you knew nothing about women.

Mr. MAY. Nothing whatever, it seems. I have been learning, yesterday and to-day, though.

Miss LITTELL. You poor fellow! the primer is blotted with tears, I am afraid. And you think now that Elizabeth did love you?

Mr. MAY. Mary told me last night that she did.

Miss LITTELL. Told you that Elizabeth loved you?

Mr. MAY (*bitterly*). Yes; she seemed to think it would give me pleasure to hear that she had *won* me, as it were. She said that Elizabeth's remark had been made playfully, in answer to some teasing allusions, but that it had not deceived her. She had guessed the truth from the first. She told me all this in a kind of triumph; it was horrible. I broke away from her, and rushed out of the house. If she had confessed it to me in repentance, if she had been anything but radiantly triumphant and laughing, I could have borne it — have forgiven it.

Miss LITTELL (*after a pause*). There is but one thing for you to do, of course.

Mr. MAY (*eagerly*). What?

Miss LITTELL. You have broken your engagement with Mary. Elizabeth is a pearl among women.

Mr. MAY. I know what you mean; but how is it possible?

Miss LITTELL. Why impossible? You love her?

Mr. MAY. Who?

Miss LITTELL. Elizabeth.

Mr. MAY. That is just what I came to ask you?

Miss LITTELL. You came to ask *me* if you loved Elizabeth?

Mr. MAY. Yes; which woman do I love? I pledge you my honour — if I have a shred of it left — that I do not know. I have not broken my engagement with Mary yet; I have not seen her since yesterday. When I think of her moral perversion, her inability to see her almost crime, I am filled with horror. And then I think of her — well, you see I have been engaged to her for a month. There is a great deal I could never forget; I 've been in a fool's paradise.

Miss LITTELL. And Elizabeth, whom you have loved so long, who is — Robert, you know what she is. Think what it would mean to live out your life with her!

Mr. MAY. Ah, do I not know! You can tell me nothing of her. I know that I love her, that I worship her; and yet — I am an absolute scoundrel; I love them both; I told you so in the beginning.

Miss LITTELL. And you told me you liked cream in

your tea in the beginning, also. Be advised; you will never forget this act of Mary's.

Mr. MAY. No, never; nor her, either.

Miss LITTELL. Then, if that is the way you feel toward Mary, by all means marry her.

Mr. MAY. When I adore the ground another woman walks on — love and respect the very hem of her gown!

Miss LITTELL (*impatiently*). Robert, would you mind calling the object of your adoration Ma-Beth for convenience sake? My brain whirls in this confusion. I 'm but a woman, you know, and the mind masculine has phases which I cannot grasp. I really think Brigham Young is the only person who could offer you any practical advice. If he met many like you I don't wonder at his conclusions.

Mr. MAY (*humbly*). Go on; I deserve it all.

Miss LITTELL (*somewhat softened*). Well, in your case, perhaps I should be equally foolish. My mother asked me yesterday whether she should buy me a red or a blue skirt, and I knew myself well enough to say, "Either; for whichever you get I shall wish I had the other." I fear it will be the same with you.

Mr. MAY. I wish this were no more serious than a mere choice of petticoats.

Miss LITTELL. Why, I thought a choice of petticoats was just the question. No; forgive me. I should not have laughed — it was flippant.

Mr. MAY (*wearily*). There is nothing to forgive. We understand each other. You have been kinder than I deserved; but I must work it out alone. (*He rises and takes her hand, holding it in his as he speaks.*) Good-night. Try not to think too badly of me, and remember, whatever happens, our friendship stands.

Miss LITTELL (*earnestly*). Good-night, and do *you* remember that I know and trust perfectly you and your honour. Whatever you decide to do, that shall I approve. Good-night.

(*As Mr.* MAY *leaves the room she sits listening to his retreating footsteps, and leans her head on her hand in deep thought.*)

Miss LITTELL (*sola*). "*Our friendship stands.*" Why did he say that? Was there a question of it in his mind? (*She pauses, and then springs to her feet with sudden vehemence.*) I have been an abject fool. I should have stopped his first words. When a man has once wept upon a handkerchief, what use has he for it again? And a handkerchief I have been to-night. Whichever girl he marries, he will hate me. I know too much. (*She looks forlornly at the empty bench with a little gesture of renunciation.*) No; this is not good-night, Robert; it is good-by.

CURTAIN.

NED.

NED.

"AND so, dear, you have decided to name the baby Ned! Was Fred quite willing?"

"It was his own suggestion. Please like it, Elizabeth."

"I do like it, little one; I love it, and I love Fred for suggesting it."

As I stood looking at the pretty maternal picture of my sister Barbara adoring her first-born, my heart was full of thankfulness and my eyes were wet with tears. "Ah, my little man," I said, stooping to kiss the tiny scrap of humanity, "if you are brought up as I think you will be, you shall be more proud of your first name than of your last. How you came by it is almost like a story." And then I suddenly thought that, perhaps, it was a story; so here it is.

"Blessed is the man that hath his quiver full of them," saith the Psalmist, and I think that even had my father been less happy in his family relations, he would have striven to feel "blessed," in order to fulfil the Scriptures. For there were twelve of us, all high-spirited and running over with mischief. I, Elizabeth, was the eldest daughter, and Barbara, who was ten years younger, the most beautiful and the favourite.

Why none of us were jealous of Barbara, I am sure I do not know; perhaps it was because we all united in spoiling her. She was the only delicate baby my mother ever had, and this naturally caused a difference in the beginning; but had it not been this, some other reason would have presented itself.

Winning ways were not lacking in Barbara, and as child and woman she was most perfectly beautiful in face and form, although some few, who had not fallen under the witchery of her personality, maintained that she was too small, too fairylike,—that the soft golden hair was too fluffy and luxuriant.

Small Barbara might be, but the erect little body was the storage-house of a spirit and fire sufficient for a dozen ordinary mortals. Her pretty, imperious ways gained for her the title of "Princess" with father and the boys. My mother disliked the name, thinking it not good for Barbara; and we girls never used it, for quite another reason. It was our small and only stand against the absolute monarchy.

But when she was about four years old, another subject was added to Barbara's list,—one who was to outstrip all others in loyal devotion; and this was Ned,—black, savage, untamable Ned.

His mother was a full-blooded African who had been purchased by our uncle, the owner of a large plantation in Virginia. He bought her with her baby in her arms, from pure compassion, he said; for she was as untamed as a savage, and evidently untamable,—utterly useless to her Florida master, who was trying to subdue her by methods of which we were spared the recital. But the change of masters came to her too late; though her spirit was unbroken, it was so bruised and festered as to render her death no surprise when it occurred some months later.

The child, whose name was Ned, was brought up in the quarters with the other negro children. He developed early a wild and lawless spirit; and when he was put into the field to work, the overseer complained constantly that he was a leader among the slaves and, thoroughly insubordinate. My uncle's attention thus called in his direction, he found Ned a man of twenty-two years, superbly built and apparently as complete a savage as his mother.

Remembering her history, my uncle determined to make no attempt to break the lad's spirit. He wrote at once to my mother, telling her the whole story and saying that as he found Ned responded to kindness, he felt sure that there was the making of a magnificent servant in him. He ended by begging my mother to accept him, and give him the individual attention that his bachelor home could not afford, adding that if the boy proved too much for her, he could be returned.

Mother and father talked the matter over; and the end of it was, Ned came. He was almost a giant, quite six feet four, but too perfectly proportioned to show his full height, and lithe and active as a panther.

My mother decided to train him as a waiter. He learned rapidly; and though at first he lifted barrels of flour with ease and trembled under a glass of water, he soon waited with a really stately elegance. The strangeness of the new home and surroundings kept the old lawless spirit in check; but familiarity bred the usual contempt, and in a few weeks Ned was king of the kitchen as absolutely as he had been king of the Virginia plantation.

Possibly this spirit was an inheritance, undoubtedly his appearance bore out the supposition; and perhaps from the same source sprang the wild gusts of rage which seemed to possess him and sweep him along resistlessly. Mother remonstrated gently, then sternly and repeatedly, all in vain.

Pandemonium seemed to have broken loose in the region below stairs. Early one morning the climax came. An uproar such as never was heard before rose from the kitchen, causing my father's hasty appearance there for the first time in many years. Huddled in one corner were the frightened negroes, and in the centre of the room towered Ned, holding the group in subjection; some trifle had irritated him, and this was the consequence.

Father was beyond measure angry,—so angry that Ned's rage paled before his. He told the rather sobered negro that he would stand no more; kindness had failed with him, and he should now have the whipping he richly deserved.

"Not to be given by me, however," he added; "the constable shall do it, and I mean to send for him to take you away at once."

So saying, my father left the house in a white heat. But he was unused to interfering in what he considered his wife's department, and was also a man of quick wrath and quicker forgetfulness; and becoming absorbed in important matters of business, he spent no further thought on Ned or his misconduct.

It was not thus at home. So severe a measure had never before been resorted to, and we were all unhappy.

Mother alone, and probably because she knew what manner of man our father was, remained as placid as ever, as she sat in the nursery sewing.

Her placidity was to be rudely interrupted. There was a sudden patter of feet in the hall, a scramble up the stairway, and Aunt Tilly, the black cook and whilom ruler of the kitchen, rushed into the room.

"Dat nigger gwine ter kill somebody yit!" she wailed. "He done shet hise'f up in de garret wid de meat-axe and ole marse's razor, an' he got all de knives what he wor a-cleanin', an' he say dar sha'n' be no po' white trash sont fer to whip him; dat he gwine ter kill de fust pusson dat set foot over de do' sill."

Two bright, hard spots of colour rose in my mother's cheeks as she listened; but her manner was unhurried as she quilted her needle into her work, and shook off the threads from her dress into the open fireplace. With her usual even pace she walked out of the room and up the stairway, we children, with the servants who had gathered in the hall, stringing after her. On she went to the partially closed garret-door; there she paused.

"Ned."

There was no answer.

Raising her hand, my mother struck the door lightly with her palm, throwing it wide open, and disclosing Ned, who stood before it. All the savage was up and looking out of the dark, scowling face, the bloodshot eyes, the drawn lips. His body was thrown back, and in one hand, raised above his head, he held the axe, in the other flashed the razor.

The servants crowded behind each other with smothered cries; but mother, with her beautiful, proud head thrown back stepped over the threshold. She was slightly and delicately made, yet, as she stood opposite the huge negro, her figure drawn up to its full height, her cheeks brilliant, her eyes flashing defiance into his, she rose above the question of brawn and muscle to become his full equal in power,—but no more.

The inflexible blue eyes and the passionate black ones looked unflinchingly into each other for what seemed to me an age. And then suddenly my mother's whole figure seemed to relax; the scornful, curling lips half smiled; the blue eyes looked infinitely soft and pitying. She stepped swiftly to Ned's side, and laid her gentle hand on his shoulder.

"You poor boy," she said softly, "why will you do so?"

Wonder drove passion from the dark face; wonder held Ned spellbound, as my mother took the weapons from his unresisting hands. But when she bade him return to his work, he seemed to awake, and darting a furious glance around, he rushed headlong from the room and down the stairs. Then something happened which I cannot think of even now without a darting sense of horror. Half-way up the stairs stood little Barbara; her nurse had deserted her, and she was following after.

Spreading out her tiny arms, she blocked Ned's way. "You is dot to tarry me down 'tairs," she cried in her sweet treble. "I hurted my foot, and I are n't a-doin' to walk."

Ned stopped and hesitated. I sprang forward, but mother, her face as pale as her kerchief, held my arm in an iron grasp. I turned sick and faint; everything swam before my eyes, and when I could see again, it was a strange sight that awaited me. Barbara was sitting high in Ned's arms, singing a little tune to herself, and beating time upon his woolly head.

He carried her down the stairs, straight to the wood-room, where they spent the rest of the morning. One minute Ned was sawing wood furiously, and the next he was sitting with Barbara on his knee, delighting her heart by strange stories and games. Mother made me peep in occasionally, but would not allow them to be disturbed.

"The child is doing him good," she said.

At last the nursery door opened softly, and Ned entered with Barbara cradled in his arms sound asleep. He laid her in the crib, covering her carefully, tenderly soothing her when she half woke, and then left the room with noiseless step.

The battle was over. Ned had found his master, and that master was a baby.

There was never any real trouble with Ned after this. He now had a motive for good behaviour, and lived in deadly fear of being sent back to Virginia, away from "de fiddle-string of his heart, his Miss Princess."

When he felt his old rages coming on, he used simply to depart, where, we never knew; sometimes he was gone for one day, sometimes for two. My mother wisely forebore asking questions; and when we children did so, he would invariably reply gravely,—

"I was sont fur suddint to go to the Islant of Dardanelles fur to wait on my Lord Concarson."

Barbara never had one atom of curiosity, so she never inquired unless we put her up to it; but even then we got no satisfaction. Ned would pick her up and carry her off, saying,—

"Yes, honey; Ned 's gwine to tell Miss Princess all 'bout it, — jes' you come wid me."

But on her return we could never gather that she knew any more than we did; Barbara was so easily distracted, and so lacking in any desire for knowledge.

In one respect Ned was very considerate. He never disappeared if guests were expected, and on one occasion he even returned hastily on remembering a dinner-party.

"Jes' s'pose I hed 'a' gone on disrememberin' dis here party," I heard him say to Aunt Tilly. "Dere ain' one o' you niggers as knows how even to set de table, and when it come to waitin' — Lord! I jes' run back like a har soon as I come to think 'bout it. I ain' stop to take breff."

But these departures became less and less frequent, as his adoration of Barbara grew stronger.

It was a strange sight to see the two together. Barbara's manner was as if graciously permitting affection, while Ned's was that of actual worship. Her first remark on seeing him was always, "I wants to be tarried;" and Ned knew no higher happiness than holding her curled up in his great arm.

I think she enjoyed the sense of his powerful strength. A great deal of his work was done thus encumbered; but as Ned could set a table better with one hand than any one else with two, he was allowed to do as he chose.

He was Barbara's willing slave, — a slave whom no Emancipation Act could liberate, though Ned himself was a great Abolitionist, and fond of making speeches upon the subject in the kitchen. My father had some misgivings about slave-holding also; and I think Ned divined the truth when he said; —

"Ole Mass', he done give Aunt Tilly her freedom for

a Christmas gif'. I guess his cornscience been a-bearin' down on him."

But, however undecided were my father's politics, Ned's opinions were very definitely settled; and yet one small incident that occurred in the first year of our Civil War was to make him bitterly opposed to all that he had previously held dear.

When the war broke out, Barbara was eight years old, and going to school with me. I was to leave at the end of the year. Our city was on the border line and constantly full of soldiers; so my mother preferred to send Ned to and from school with us. But one day we were dismissed a few minutes earlier than usual, and I started home alone with my little sister.

When only a square from our door, we met a Union soldier walking toward us. He looked admiringly at Barbara, and then stopped.

"Will you give me a kiss, my pretty bird?" he said.

Barbara shrank to my side, speechless with terror. I do not believe the man meant to frighten her; he was a mild-looking little fellow, and probably had children of his own at home; but he stopped and lifted Barbara high in the air to steal the wished-for kiss.

That kiss he never got; for she was suddenly seized and whisked out of his hands and over his head, to his infinite astonishment. Ned was on the way to meet us, and had flown to the rescue.

It was well for the little soldier, and perhaps well for Ned also, that Barbara required all of her faithful servant's soothing and attention. But from that moment Ned's horror of "dem Yanks" knew no bounds; and hatred of them included a hatred of their principles. His speeches in the kitchen veered in doctrine with an alarming suddenness.

He had things his own way, as usual; for the men were afraid of him, and the maids admired him. Aunt Tilly alone spoke her mind, and I heard her do it from my up-stairs window.

"You was a-talkin' de oder side of yer mouf," she said, as she hopped up and down in her vain endeavour to throw a dripping sheet over the high clothes-line in the yard. "You was a-sayin' dere warn't no right in a-holdin' de slaves."

Ned took the sheet from her with a contemptuous kindness, and slung it over the line.

"Dat was before I knowed," he answered coolly; and then, emphasizing his remark by driving down the clothes-pins, he added impressively, "*dat's* what niggers was made fur."

The year 1865 was soon to prove that Ned and many others were mistaken. But we children cared little for this or anything else that did not directly concern us; and so the years of childhood slipped away with only enough shadow about them to throw out the sunlight more strongly, and when Barbara's seventeenth birthday came it was to find us children yet in many ways. Barbara was still the "Princess," and Ned was, if possible, more than ever her captive. The great change was that Barbara was engaged to be married, and engaged to a Northerner who had lately settled among us, — a Mr. Damer, soon known to all of us as "Fred;" for formality was not possible with one of his sunny nature and kind heart.

Except for her extreme youth, I think we all were satisfied with Barbara's engagement, Ned alone excepted.

That Barbara should marry anybody was bad enough; but that she should marry one of "dem Yanks" was intolerable.

He waited on Fred at table with undisguised disgust, muttering and shaking his head behind his back at every opportunity, invariably beginning to wait on him from the right side, and just as Fred adjusted himself to the awkwardness, rushing around to the left. It really amounted to a petty persecution, which kept the children in delighted spasms of laughter and me in misery. My mother could not see from behind her tea-urn what was going on, and my father never saw or heard anything. But at last Ned undertook to slap down as a gauntlet each plate and dish before his foe, and his mutterings began to grow audible. One day, on seeing Fred pay some little attention to mother, he spoke too loud for further ignoring.

"I sees yer, I sees yer, 'deed I does; throwing cobs at the cow, is yer? Yes, to make de ca'f take notice. Yer don' git dis yer ca'f, ef Ned kin help it, — naw, sir."

This was too much; my patience was exhausted, and I complained to father.

At the next meal my remonstrance took effect. Just as Ned was indulging in an unusually horrible contortion of his visage, and as my delighted brother John was stuffing all of his handkerchief into his mouth, my father looked up suddenly, and bent his white brows on Ned until they met in a straight line over his blue eyes. Thus he continued to gaze at him until the embarrassed negro managed to get himself out of the room. Then turning to the now sober John, father significantly motioned to the door, through which the scared boy escaped, glad to get off so easily.

My father never used unnecessary words; and as he knew none were needed to meet this occasion, none were said, and at least outward peace reigned until the first lover's quarrel arose. Then Ned was one broad grin; he seemed to scent danger for the hated intruder, and he hung about Barbara, perfectly happy in the fact that she, as in her childish troubles, seemed to prefer his constant attendance to anything else.

I was never quite able to make out what this quarrel was about, though it lasted several days; but it was not difficult to see that Barbara was behaving like the spoiled baby she was, and that Fred was very patient, — more patient than I for him, for at last, finding Barbara alone in the library, I administered the good round scolding that I thought she needed. Unused as she was to any harshness, it did not take long to reduce her to floods of tears; and she was sobbing her heart out apparently, when Fred entered the room.

As I closed the library door behind me two minutes after his entrance, it was with the fixed opinion, which I have seen no reason to alter since, that the male or female who attempts to interfere with even the potentially married is a fool. What conclusions the lovers came to in their prolonged reconciliation, I do not know. When we all met in the drawing-room in the evening, Barbara appeared her old bewitching self, supremely happy and contented. What arguments had been used to work the change, I never asked, and Barbara never told me. However it may have been, the result was satisfactory.

Fred was a trifle more communicative, but indirectly. Taking me into a corner later in the evening, he gravely inquired if I thought my father would object to his taking Ned out into the yard and wringing his neck.

"If he did not, Barbara would," I replied. "What has poor Ned been doing now?"

"Poor Ned, indeed! He has been abusing me as usual. I was at my innocent devotions this afternoon, worshipping at my shrine in the attitude common to worshippers of every faith and clime, when he attacked me. Elizabeth, being behind the scenes, why did you not intercept the afternoon tea-tray brought in by Ned with catlike step, and handed to Barbara over my devoted head and prostrate form? I had two horrible alternatives: to rise suddenly to my feet, thereby upsetting the tray and all its contents, or to crab out sidewise. I chose the latter, and even as I emerged, was offered tea by my tormentor with respectful gravity."

"What did Barbara do?" I asked, laughing heartily.

"Why, Barbara came to my rescue nobly. She reproved Ned scathingly, and with the air of an insulted princess, for putting only one lump of sugar in her tea — I think that was it."

"Reproved Ned, and before you!" I cried. "Then, indeed, she punished him. The jealous hatred he bears you is beyond words. My impression is that he is not going to put up with your presence much longer. I have been for some time expecting a message for Ned from Lord Concarson, necessitating a voyage to the Island of the Dardanelles."

"Not he!" cried Fred. "No such luck for poor me!"

I was nearer right than I thought. The next morning brought with it the news that Ned was off again, and with no farewell message except a box of dainty candies tied to Barbara's door-knob.

We thought a couple of days at most would see Ned in his place again. But no — Barbara had gone over to the enemy; his own eyes had seen incontestable proof of a complete reconciliation. It was not to be borne, and shaking the dust from his feet, Ned departed in earnest.

Perhaps it was for the best. Barbara missed him sadly and grieved long over his absence, repenting often her hasty words. But, as the days went by, she grew more and more absorbed in her lover, and I do not think Ned's jealous heart could have borne the sight. And when Barbara's wedding day came, and our clinging little Princess was taken from us, I thought of Ned and rejoiced in his absence, believing that his undisciplined nature would have suffered a pang ten times sharper than mine.

But Barbara had not seen her faithful servant for the last time; she was soon to meet him again. And of this meeting I have heard the story so often, that it has grown impossible for me to feel that I was not there in person, so I shall tell it as if such were the fact.

Fred and Barbara seemed inclined to spend the rest of their lives in one prolonged wedding journey. Every day they determined to set their faces toward home to-morrow, and each to-morrow found them lingering. Drifting about in this way, they strolled one noon into the dining-room of a New York hotel, and sat awaiting their luncheon. The waiters were all negroes; and as Barbara idly looked at them, thinking how natural their dusky faces appeared to her Southern eyes, her attention was caught by something familiar in the figure of the headwaiter, whose back was toward her. Suddenly he turned, and Ned and his "Miss Princess" were face to face.

In the joy of that meeting, even the man who had stolen his treasure was forgiven. He had no words too eloquent to express his passionate delight, no entreaties too urgent to implore their stay. The best that the hotel could offer was theirs, and no hands but Ned's were allowed to proffer the dishes. Barbara's happiness was but little less than his; and when they left the dining-room after the prolonged meal, it was with the promise to make their stay an extended one. With this understanding, Ned bade them a reluctant farewell for the afternoon.

But in an hour or so a message was brought to him that Mrs. Damer wished to see him in her sitting-room. He found her alone, lying in a corner of her couch, looking pale and suffering.

"Ah, Ned," she cried, as he entered; "my head does ache so! I have been to see Aunt Mary, and she keeps her house as hot here as she did when she lived at home. It made me so ill, — just as it used to!"

Ned was all tender sympathy. She was his little mistress once more, and he was her great, gentle nurse. He brought her a cup of strong tea made by his own hands. Had she asked for nightingale's tongues, he would have produced them somehow. Barbara sipped the fragrant tea, and listened to the familiar voice, contentedly.

"Ned," she said, looking up at him suddenly, "why did you run away?"

For a moment Ned's composure failed him, and his eyes dropped; then a smile crept over his face.

"Yer see, honey," he said, "I was jest 'bleeged to go. My Lord Concarson, he don' sen' fur dis nigger deep in de night an' all de way from de Islant of Dardanelles lessen he means business. I did n't even have de time fur to say good-by to my pretty baby."

Barbara listened with soft laughter. "Ned," she said, "tell me about the Island of Dardanelles."

Ned obediently began a long fallacious tale of a lovely, lonely land, — a land of tropic growth and splendour. The story was such as he had told Barbara over and over again in her baby days. Gradually her eyelids sleepily drooped and fell, opened, drooped again, and then under the spell of the familiar phrases she fell asleep.

The dining-room of the hotel where Ned was in charge was somewhat apart from the rest of the building, and this probably was the last place where the alarm of fire was heard when it broke out in the hotel, not an hour after Ned had left Barbara's side. His first thought was for her safety; and he rushed from the dining-room, through the hall, and up the main stairway which led to her rooms.

The hallways were full of screaming women and children, and were thick with smoke; great clouds were rolling in from every side. On the first landing Ned met Barbara's husband, a baby in either arm, and a half fainting woman clinging to his shoulder.

"Miss Princess!" gasped Ned.

"Safe," was the laconic answer, as Fred bundled the babies into Ned's arms and caught the tottering woman.

The fire had been smouldering too long before being discovered to think of saving much more than human life now that the flames had broken out, and it required brave and determined efforts to accomplish even this. At last the order was issued by the captain of the fire-brigade that no one should further risk life and limb by re-entering the doomed building. Ned had been foremost among the workers, and he now prepared to enjoy himself.

An African is always a voluptuary in his pleasures; and, abandoning himself with true negro delight to the sway of excitement, Ned drifted about with the seething and twisting of the crowd, until he found himself standing close by Fred's side. He then resisted the pressure which was bearing him forward, and spoke reproachfully, —

"I jes' hope you got Miss Princess a-lookin' at dis yer fire from somewhar. She allays did love a fire. Many 's de one I done tuk her toe outen de back gate when ole Miss think she war in de nuss'ry an' I war in de woodhus. Thar war n't none on it she did n't see, a-settin' up on my shoulder an' crowin' like a little rooster. Ole Miss, she cot me takin' her onct. Lord, but she did raise! I disremember jes' what she tol' me, but I know I ain' tuk de chile no mo'. Ho, ho!"

Fred listened with much amusement.

"I am afraid your Miss Barbara cannot see this fire from where she is," he said; "I took her across the city early this afternoon to visit her aunt. It is not my fault that she is not with me; they did n't want me, and told me so."

"An' yer ain' seen Miss Princess sence de fire bruk out?"

"No — for God's sake, man, what is the matter with you?"

The two faces looked into each other, a strange contrast, — one with staring white eyeballs and eyes full of a horrible intelligence, the other white and ghastly with its dawning terror.

No further words were needed. Both men turned and sprang forward as moved by one muscle; but the action of the negro was with hand and foot. A well-directed blow from his ponderous fist made the husband of his young mistress stagger; and when he recovered his footing Ned had gained the moment's advantage, and was cleaving his way through the crowd, which opened for him as did the Red Sea for Moses, — "a wall on the right hand and on the left."

As he reached the door of the burning building, his path was barred by a fireman in his full panoply and power of office.

"Git out, ye black fool," he shouted, in unmistakable Irish.

Out swept that powerful black arm, and with what seemed but a gesture, the burly Irishman was brushed aside. The next moment Ned was up the deserted stairway, and had gained the first landing. Here he paused. There was no one now to bar his progress but Death clad in his most fearful terrors.

The negro stooped and began to draw off his boots. The stairway hung by a thread, and his step must be catlike. He cast one look back into the surging mass of life below, and saw there a man struggling vainly in the grasp of a dozen hands. He heard a hoarse voice crying, —

"Curse you, let me go; my wife is in that hell!"

Above the roar of the fire, above the shout of many voices, rose the stentorian tones of the captain of the brigade, —

"Hold on to him, boys! Hold on to him! There 's one chance in a hundred, and that hangs on those steps. There sha'n't be a foot set on 'em."

Ned heard, saw, and was satisfied that the first part of his mission was accomplished. He set his bared foot on the charred steps, and began the ascent, the first turn hiding him from the eyes of the crowd below.

A death-like silence fell on the multitude, — a silence rendering more horribly audible the resistless, sullen roar of the fire, which licked and curled about the eaves of the house, and which the hissing water seemed but to feed. Great tongues of flame broke from one window and another, as if the devouring fiends within were looking out deridingly at the white, upturned faces. A woman's hysterical sobs alone broke the stillness, and she was sternly hushed.

Barbara's husband ceased to struggle in the firemen's grasp.

Have you ever known what waiting means, — known more than its impatient restlessness? Have you ever felt that stopping of the heart's pulses for one moment of anxious listening, and then at some sound the wild rush and thunder of the blood in your veins, the agony of the clutch at your very life and being, your breath stopped in your throat? If you have never known all this, you have never known waiting, and you may pray Heaven to spare you that knowledge. This suffering and this knowledge are Frederic Damer's.

Crash!

A cry rose from the listening crowd in answer to the sound, and the woman who had sobbed before was carried away fainting.

"Thank God, it 's only the lower stairway gone!" said the captain; "the landing still holds. I can reach it with a ladder; get me one."

"I go with you," said a quiet, determined voice beside him; it was Barbara's husband.

The captain turned and looked at him closely; apparently what he saw satisfied him.

"Yes, sir," he answered calmly. "Give him your helmet, Jack. We must go now, sir; I hear them on the stair."

They entered the burning house together; at any moment the roof might fall. Four lives were now in jeopardy where two had stood before. The sound of a footfall slowly became an established fact.

"That ain't but one person walking, sir," said the captain, gently, "and you'd best not hope, for that foot's bare."

"Then he is carrying her," said Fred; and again nothing but the dread fire sounds and that stealthy footfall broke the silence.

At last! at last! Out of the smoke, out of the flame, on to the frail platform stepped the gigantic negro, his clothing literally torn and burned from his body, the blood streaming from a ghastly wound in his head, his breath coming in sobs like those of a wounded stag; but in his arms, gathered close to his breast, her fair curls gleaming on its blackness, lay the unconscious form of his Miss Princess.

Once more he was carrying her safely home from a fire, and now, indeed, for the last time! By the help of the two waiting men the descent of the ladder was made, and Barbara lay in her husband's arms. Even at this supreme moment, he observed with a rush of grateful emotion that the blanket in which she was swathed had been saturated in water.

As the rescuer and the rescued passed out from the blazing house, a wild shout burst from the excited crowd, which pressed forward beyond control. But even as his dimmed sense heard the cries, as the blessed air of heaven smote upon him, Ned staggered and dropped to the ground. The blood gushed out from his ears and mouth; he was picked up by strong hands and carried into a neighbouring house, where at least there were quiet and care.

In another room in the same building Barbara lay, still unconscious; but the swoon caused by fright and shock soon yielded to treatment, and she awoke, crying hysterically for "Mother!" and clinging nervously to her husband.

But her first fully conscious thought was for Ned. Fred could not command his voice to answer her eager, persistent questions, and it was the physician in charge who gently broke to her the news of his danger, and who left her to seek the latest report of his condition.

In these few moments, alone with the wife "brought to him like Alcestis from the grave," I think we may forgive a brief forgetfulness of the Hercules whose gift she was; but it was with a sense of remorseful awakening that Fred looked at the grave face of the physician as he entered, saying, "I can give you but little encouragement."

"Oh, no, no!" cried Barbara; "you can, you must save him! Go to him, both of you. I promise to be perfectly quiet; I won't move, — only go, oh, go!"

As the door closed behind the two men, Fred turned to the physician with an inquiring look, and was answered by a shrug of the shoulders and an outward motion of the hands more expressive than any words. Everything that skill could do had been done, but from the first it needed no medical verdict to tell that there was no hope.

Ned did not seem to suffer, but lay almost unconscious, breathing heavily. Fred, bending over him in an agony of grateful pity, saw his lips move, and bending nearer, thought he heard him whisper, "Miss Princess."

"Shall I bring her to you?" he asked, and waiting for no answer, went hastily for his wife.

She started up with eager eyes as he entered. "Is there no hope?" she cried.

"There has been none from the first," he answered. "Dear, he is asking for you. Can you bear it? There is not a moment to lose."

"Oh, take me to him quickly, quickly."

He lifted her tenderly, and half led, half carried her to the room of the dying man. But in his short absence there had been a change in the sufferer; agony had partially restored consciousness, and each breath was a moan.

"Come, Lord, come! Oh, Lord, come git me!" he was crying feebly as they entered the room.

"Love, it is too late. You may not stay now; he would not wish it."

But Barbara broke from her husband's detaining arm, and threw herself on her knees by Ned's bedside.

Her presence seemed to rouse him. He opened his eyes and looked at her tearful face. "'T ain't so terrible bad, darlin'," he gasped brokenly. "I ain't a-cryin' none, — jis' whisperin' to de Lord, honey, jis' whisperin' to de Lord."

Barbara buried her face in the bedside and burst into a passion of tears. He husband stepped forward to draw her away, fearing that she might disturb the dying man;

but Ned seemed to divine his intention, and rallying his strength, laid a detaining hand on her sunny curls, raising her face to his sight.

"Don' take on so, darlin'," he whispered; "I 's got to go, but I ain' goin' fur, honey, not to say fur." A gleam of the old humour shot across his face. "Ned only gwine to the Islant of Dardenelles, honey, fur to wait on my Lord Con —"

A sudden shudder shook his whole frame; his face was contorted in agony. Barbara's husband laid his hand quickly across her eyes to shut out the sight.

And when he drew it away again all was over; Ned had at last made his voyage to the Blessed Isles, and was waiting upon his Lord — whose name was not Concarson.

"THROUGH A GLASS, DARKLY."

"THROUGH A GLASS, DARKLY."

TO-MORROW I enter into my new life; to-morrow I leave my past behind me forever. To-day I am — well, what I am; to-morrow I shall be known as "the wife of Senator Blythe," and after that as a Power. Power! there is indefinable force in the very sound of the word. Power: I like to say it over.

Come here, my little mirror. Sit on the table by me, and let us have an honest talk, you and I; it is long since I have talked honestly to any one. You are the only article of real value on my dressing-table. My brush has a wooden back; my comb is of india-rubber. Ah, well, all that will be changed to-morrow; but now you alone are suited to me. Ivory, tipped with gold — a gift of Emily's; the frame painted by herself, — passion-flowers: they look like her. This dainty, delicately tinted corner might be Emily herself. But let us talk, — we two. It is the last time I shall ever see you, my dear. Suppose we look each other squarely in the face before we say good-by.

And so this is what I have fought the battle with — and won. I am not beautiful, — not as Emily was. I know that my hair and eyes are superb, but the rest of my face is open to criticism. How has it been that at twenty-four, with this, my only stock-in-trade, to back me, I have played for a high stake — and won?

We know, do we not, my mirror? As we speak of it now "the old Circe looks from out my eyes."

Yes, that was it: I knew my power; .but it had to be used with caution. It is easy for such a woman, alone in the world, to be called an adventuress. I was clever enough to escape that; no one ever called me that but once — and the poor little woman was hounded to it. I shall never forget that day by the sea. How her baby-face quivered when she found us alone on the rocks, and how her eyes flashed through her tears!

"Adventuress!"

I can hear her now. She had her bitterness to bear, and she gave me mine. I liked her spirit, but it stung all the same. I remember how I sat, white and silent, catching my breath from the force of the blow. What a brute her husband showed himself! He spoke to her as my husband will never speak to me; or if he does, the woman in question will not get off so easily as I did. She came to heel at once, poor little thing, and apologized to the "unfriended, lonely woman she had insulted." I was always a fool about those pretty baby-women. I should not have made a bad man, I think; as a woman, I am a mistake. When I took the hand she gave me at her husband's command, I hated him. How I should have liked to advise her a little! but I paid off her score for her,— paid it in full. Ah, my young friend, you were a little astonished the next day when I dropped my pathetic rôle, and told you with point-blank coolness that you loved me. I laughed in his face, told him to look into his heart, and see what I saw there. I had only played with him for an hour, because I foolishly fancied that his eyes were like others I had known,—like those clear, honest, trusting eyes which should have been difficult for dishonest ones to meet,—but not for mine. He went back to his child-wife cured, but a man, not the boy he had been; he will never be that again. If any mother wanted her son matured, I think I could guarantee to do it in two weeks—certainly three.

I must be careful not to smile like that; it does not suit my style, does it, my faithful friend? Or perhaps suits it too well? I was very near trying to deceive you; you just caught me in time. You see, it comes naturally to me; it was the bread-and-milk of my baby-days: "Mamma, mamma, pretty mamma,—I want to be with my mamma."

Charming maternal picture!—with the pathetic widow's weeds as background. I played my part with great spirit for such a tiny thing; it was not my fault that the child-lover retired without results. As the next on the carpet hated children, I was banished to the nursery, and later to boarding-school, where I studied because I chose to, and not because of good teaching. I gained other things there too,—my power of apparent self-effacement, of stern self-control, of close watchfulness; and there, later, came Emily,—beautiful, dignified, wealthy. I made up my mind that she should love me; and I easily accomplished this, she was so loving and unsuspecting. I went to her English home with her from school,—as I meant to. Ah, those two months, those halcyon days!—in them I learned the fascination I possessed; in them I learned to use it. Emily might be beautiful,—was beautiful,—pure, and exquisite as the lining of a shell, but, beside me, she who had everything was as nothing.

Not in *his* eyes alone, but in the eyes of others. I saw it plainly; had I not, everything might have been different. I discovered that most women must exert themselves; I had but to be—and I was only eighteen.

And yet Emily was beautiful, beautiful. He had loved her before I came—but then!

Ah, that winding, moonlit river, those shaded walks, those tender words and tenderer caresses! His mere presence an exquisite consciousness, his absence an aching hunger!

Richard! Richard! Ah, God, if I had died in your arms that day six years ago! What! tears? One—two—three—four of them. Crocodile! Always deceitful, and striving now to deceive yourself, as you did him. Deceiving him, with his passionate kisses still warm on your lips!

"Marry you, dear? Never, never! Could I, of all women, break Emily's heart?"

Bah! what did I care for Emily? Not a snap of my fingers.

Marry him? No, no! Not the young country squire, with his estate smothered in mortgages, in spite of his brave pink coat and blooded horses. I found all that out, and despised myself for doing so. But I collected my facts first, and did the despising afterwards; one generally does. I took the first-fruits of my heart, and offered them to my Moloch of ambition; to-morrow I get my reward.

I had a small sum of money of my own, and had been adding to it by writing; my pen was a ready, caustic one, and I could rely on it. Live with my step-father, accept his grudging charity, I found I could not. I worked hard, made for myself a position, and was known to the Press as one wielding a brilliant pen, not too scrupulous, and thoroughly useful. I saw nothing of any women; I lived alone. I knew I should never gain anything from them but a sufferance, and that was not worth working for; but with men it was different. There I had the fearlessness of certain success.

I like to think of the good offers of marriage I have refused; I consider it a remarkable circumstance that in my position I could have chosen a humdrum, respectable existence at any time. Yes, I think of it with complacency, and of my strength to say no. Do you recognize what faith in myself I must have had to do this?

What a wonderful lobbyist I was for an amateur! I had other ends in view, or I should have adopted it as a profession. I only dabbled in it for excitement; it was my absinthe. I made that clearly understood. When a case had been tried and pronounced impossible, how I enjoyed working it! When that great political move had to be made, and when Senator Blythe, the unapproachable, had to be brought to support it, who could be found to bell the cat but me? I who had nothing to lose, nothing to gain but another experience.

But he was difficult, more difficult than I could have imagined; there was nothing to catch hold of in his smooth yet grim exterior. I was courteously defeated at every point by this elderly man. He had me at a disadvantage from the first. My charm of face and manner were but so much material to be enjoyed, without moving him an iota.

I had met my match; it was like flinging flowers at a sun-dial. His course was marked out, and he would pursue it steadily. How I admired him when I arose to go, outwitted and defeated!

It was you who prompted me to turn and speak on the very threshold of the room, — you, my mocking familiar.

"Senator Blythe, although I have entirely failed in what I came to accomplish, I do not feel that my visit has been for naught. I have known Senator Blythe the orator, the statesman, the author; now I know Senator Blythe the man, — the man whose personality has left me nothing to say but farewell."

Gross, crude, palpable, was it not? I waited for a sarcasm which should crush me to the earth from lips so well accustomed to that mode of warfare.

"H'm, h'm!"

Senator Blythe was pulling his collar up a little higher toward his clean-shaven chin, and waiting with open mouth for more; he got it, — of course he got it at once. I had left the beaten path to seek this powerful mind, this great leader, and behold, the old accustomed road was the only way! Old or young, grave or gay, foolish or wise, it is all the same, my mirror, and you knew it.

I did not press my advantage, — "would not trespass on his time; would he think over the matter under discussion, and confer with me at my address?"

The great political battle was won, and, with it, my own. Victory seemed to come to me by mere chance; was it chance only?

We know better than that, do we not? All great victories must seem so. None but the victor knows of the weary hours spent in preparing for the pregnant moment. It may come like a thief in the night; but it will come to him who waits and watches. The eye must be hawk-like behind its softness, the mental muscles whip-cord, the hand trained to close thus: finger by finger, slowly, stealthily, surely.

What a pretty, slim hand it is! "A curled-up rose-leaf," he used to call it. "Give me your hand, love,—those soft, rosy tips. Let me kiss them, finger by finger; and now one for the palm." Let me listen a moment, only a moment.

Clinging kisses they must have been to be there still. Ah, Richard! "All the perfumes of Arabia will not sweeten this little hand." Yet to-morrow it will wash and be clean. Essence of Power is stronger than the perfumes of Arabia; that shall cleanse this little hand.

To-morrow I am to be myself no more. You, my friend, looking at me so closely now, will be as one dead; I shall be as a phœnix rising from my ashes. Every link with the past I have destroyed. Yes, I am deceiving you again—or trying to. I have not destroyed—everything; I have kept back one little relic, so small that I thought you would pass it over, but you are right to be inexorable. Here it is,—a tiny gold heart, so small that it has hung about my neck and in my bosom for six years without discovery. Never mind the contents. I will lay all in the hottest part of the fire.

Very well done indeed. One sudden kiss, your hand pressed to your side, your tears dashed away. Your eyes look very pretty and misty; that pathetic droop to the lips is becoming. Such a pity no one is here to see! All very correctly done. Tears over the first desperate lover, the first kisses; and the relics burned on the night before one's wedding!

And now, having spoken truths to you, I am going to break you into a thousand pieces and throw you away. I do not want to see you again after this. But first let me look into your eyes — soul to soul. Tell me, have you any regrets; have you any fear that you have not done wisely? Stop and think.

No, I have done well; and I am only twenty-four. I see before me a series of satisfying circumstances. I like those words; they are alliterative, too. "A series of satisfying circumstances." Satisfied ambition; satisfied pride; satisfied love of power! I know just what my statesman can give me — now and later. We can work it out together, he and I; we have already begun. And though he be fascinated, he is no hot-blooded young fool; he knows just what my help means.

Why are you looking at me with that expression? Am I still keeping something back?

Yes?

Well, take it, then. I have sacrificed my soul to my Moloch, tortured my brain, bartered my youth; and to-morrow I sell my body. To do this well, I had first to ossify my heart; and I did it quite successfully.

But there is one spot over which I can never form more than a frail crust; and sometimes it is a gaping wound so tender that even to breathe on it causes exquisite agony, and that spot is guarded by the white, set face of a young, hot-blooded fool. With clouded eyes, and lips that for six years have been saying over and over again the same words: "Farewell! farewell forever, my true darling, my brave heart! Farewell — farewell!"

And now with one crash, you and all my past life are destroyed together, and I step into my new life, clean confessed and without absolution.

To-morrow I must borrow a glass to dress my hair for my wedding; and the next day I may buy a dozen if I choose, and frame them all in gold. But not one — no, not one — shall have on it even the leaf of a passion-flower.

THE OLD PENINSULA HOUSE.

THE OLD PENINSULA HOUSE.

IT was the year of our Lord eighteen hundred and sixty. A hot September sun shone down on the South Branch of the Potomac as it ran brawling and splashing along, angrily wrestling with every obstacle that stopped its way; but wrestle as it might, a bank of stone was able to resist and turn the river out of its course, making it almost describe a circle. On the beautiful peninsula thus formed stood a square stone-house surrounded by numerous out-buildings and magnificent old trees.

The old homestead showed signs of prosperity and the utmost care in a near past; now the first pitiable marks of neglect and decay were apparent. The fences were broken; a shutter flapped on one hinge in the fitful breeze; the once clean-shaven lawn, which ran from the front of the house to the water's edge, was strewn with leaves and wore an unkempt air of litter. But if there were any human interest behind the hot eye of that September sun, it was not held by the quiet beauty of the scene, nor yet its sadness. Strange echoes and a sense of apprehension were in the air; the cattle stopped feeding and raised their heads; an old negro picking up apples straightened his back and looked about uneasily.

Suddenly a man clad in the uniform of a Confederate soldier ran with the silent rapidity of a gray squirrel over the narrow neck which bound the homestead to the mainland. He was without a hat, and his clothes were mud-stained; his breath came in laboured sighs; only an indomitable will worked the machinery of his exhausted frame.

Again the air was disturbed by pistol-shots and shouts; the loud voices grew louder, and a handful of Federal soldiers dashed across the neck. They were led by an officer whose practised eye scanned the peninsula.

"Halt!" he called; "the fool has run into a trap. Do you two guard this neck; the rest follow!"

The flying gray figure disappeared in a hedge of evergreens which separated the front lawn from the garden and cornfield at the back of the house.

"God help him! Oh, pray God help him!" pleaded Miss Etty Trot, standing at her upper window.

Her heart was beating wildly, her hands were clasped until each nail was white with the pressure, as she watched the fugitive cross the garden and run among the stubble where the corn stood in shocks.

A moment later two blue-coated figures broke through the evergreens; there was no one in sight, and they paused doubtfully.

Unable to bear the suspense, Miss Etty covered her face with her hands, and turned away trembling; sobbing like a child, she fell on her knees in an agony of prayer.

A knock at the door roused her.

"Miss Etty, honey; Miss Etty—" It was the unmistakable negro voice, inarticulate from excitement. The household was a well-trained one; under no pressure would Uncle Dan have omitted knocking at his mistress's door, although he had been her nurse in childhood, and had waited on her for more than thirty years.

"Miss Etty, a Yank cap'en in de hall, chile. He say he got ter see yer. He gwine to such de house, anyho'."

Miss Etty held her hand over her fluttering heart. Then the fugitive was not yet found! Ah, to hurry them through the house!—to get them away that she might search!

The stairway of the old mansion rose from the centre of the great square hall; it ended in a gallery which ran around all four walls, and on which the upper rooms opened. Standing at the hall-door, not only the stair but a part of the gallery could be seen.

At this point of vantage the Federal officer was stationed. The blaze of noonday light would fall on the figure whose descent he had ordered.

He saw a tiny, shrinking form appear on the gallery; it descended the steps slowly, looking at him as some startled wild creature might at its captor. Behind her shuffled Uncle Dan, equally frightened, but with a dogged faithfulness.

The small white-robed lady reached the bottom of the stair, and paused. The draught which swept the hall blew back the light hair from about her temples, and showed the fine blue veins there. A lace kerchief crossed on her bosom fluttered as though the wind had crept there also.

"Is she nineteen or thirty?" thought the man in the doorway; "one can never tell with these little light women."

The little light woman drew nearer to him, at the cost

of an effort which left no trace of blood in her cheeks; she opened her lips, but speech died in their child-like quivering.

The officer stirred uneasily; he was moved, and therefore his voice was unnecessarily stern as he demanded to be taken over the house.

Had he met with opposition, his task would have been an easier one. With growing discomfort, he followed the little figure and timid voice up and down stairways, and through room after room. His demands gradually became requests, his requests, apologies.

Dan toiled steadfastly after them, but his mistress carried her key-basket, and opened the doors with her own hands. Before one she paused and looked up appealingly, but the officer averted his eyes and the door swung open. Uncle Dan cast one scared glance into the darkened room, then turned his ashen face, puckered with rage, toward the searcher.

"Ef ole Marse warnt dade, you darsent," he snarled.

"It was my dear mother's room," said Miss Etty; "it has never been changed since she left it. Uncle Dan was very fond of her." The gentle courtesy, the note of patient pain in the soft voice, were not lost on her listener. He closed the door reverently, locked it, and laid the key in the basket on Miss Etty's arm.

"My dear young lady, I am not quite a brute," he said. "Assure me that there is no one hidden in the house, and I leave you in peace."

"No, no one," breathed she, too eagerly.

A long pause, and then: "Nor in the grounds?"

Under the keen eyes searching her face, her eyelids flickered and fell. The same pitifully frightened expression which had moved him before, crept over her features.

"It is her brother or lover, poor soul," thought the man watching her.

When Miss Etty looked up again she was alone with Dan in the great gallery; from below she heard a voice calling out quick orders, and then the regular beat of retreating footsteps. She stood with lifted head, listening; not daring to trust her ears, she climbed panting to the observatory at the top of the house, and already far down the road, her wondering eyes could distinguish the handful of Federal soldiers led by their officer.

The little woman owned a grateful heart and a soul steeped in piety.

"May the Lord bless him!" she said fervently, — "may the Lord bless him and keep him!"

Assured of safety, she ran out to the cornfield, calling with caution, but almost gayly, in her sweet high voice, —

"Soldier, soldier, you can come out now; the Yanks have gone!"

"Oh, Lord, Miss Etty, is that you?"

Miss Etty started back with a cry of alarm, for the voice had come from the ground at her feet. From out of the shock of corn by her side, peered a white face, at the sight of which, with another little cry, she sat down among the stubble. Her pretty white dress was soiled and creased as, half laughing, half sobbing, she helped to drag away the cornstalks to disclose a woful figure.

"Oh, Dick, Dick! — and I kept trying to think it was n't you."

"It 's I, all that 's left of me, Miss Etty dear."

There was not much left but undying pluck.

When Miss Etty looked at him, lying unconscious in the bed to which he was hurried, she revoked the blessing called down on his pursuer.

Six weeks before, led by his good angel, Richard McCulloch had staggered half dead into the old Peninsula House. He was wounded and ill; he was very young and dressed in rags of what had been the dearly loved gray.

These were arguments sufficient to make Miss Etty take him into her starved heart; but there was added a likeness to her brother, — the young brother who, after having been forgiven unto seventy times seven, had suddenly disappeared from among them. His sister had to bear the burden alone when death came to the Peninsula and the broken-hearted old father and mother were taken.

When the grim visitant came again searching for the stranger within her gates, Miss Etty had once more wrestled bravely with him; and this time, having the patient's strength and youth as allies, she won.

Dick, as his nurse learned to call him, was soon hobbling about, convalescent; and although he fretted not a little under his enforced inaction, the young soldier awakened life wonderfully in the old house. He laughed aloud, and amused himself by teaching his half-frightened hostess to echo it. But he was always scrupulously gentle with her; there was that about the little lady which called out a fine chivalry in men. She grew young again and quite merry by contagion, poor little soul!

Dan, the old slave, alone held morosely aloof from this new gayety. The main spring of his life had stopped with his master's death; perversity seemed now his only trait. Even to Miss Etty he yielded but grudging obedience, and to the intruder none.

It was soon after McCulloch's coming that Miss Etty began riding into town by herself when supplies were needed; and Dan was not only irritated by being left behind, but rendered suspicious and uneasy. His querulous loyalty for the old house he had served, sharpened his wits and set him watching. He was positive that the pantry was full one day when his mistress ordered her horse and rode away for the second time in a week. The old man mounted her in eloquent silence, and stood looking after the little figure swaying in the saddle under the trees which arched over the road; he turned away, shaking his head dubiously, and scowled up at the window where McCulloch sat watching the same sight. What had such as she to do with the affairs of nations?

Perhaps the vague suggestion of some such thought was floating in the old negro's mind; it was certainly in the mind of Richard McCulloch.

Miss Etty received a warm welcome from the keeper of the country-store in Rivertown, when he saw her enter his door.

"Good-morning, Miss Trot, I'm very pleased to see you to-day; but then I always am, you know. Hot day for a ride. Water? Certainly, Miss. Perhaps you would n't mind stepping into my office and helping yourself, nice and cool there. You might sit and rest a spell."

The room was crowded with the usual village loungers; and Miss Etty, threading her way through them, disappeared in the little back-office.

She shut the door after her, locked it with noiseless caution, then with a swiftness of action which betokened habit, drew a key from behind a pile of books and opened the door of a small closet; on one of its shelves lay a packet of papers and a Confederate uniform. The papers she at once disposed of by hiding them in her bosom; The uniform remained a problem. She stood with her finger on her lip, pondering. There was no one to see her, and yet as a way out of the difficulty presented itself to her mind, she blushed crimson and shrank back as though another's suggestion had shocked her sensitive maidenhood.

It was characteristic of the woman that while the hot blood was yet in her cheeks she began to divest herself of her riding-habit. The gray coat was twisted into an inglorious bustle; the cap, Miss Etty set on her head, pushing her own hat down over it, binding the shaky structure together with her thick veil. When it came to the trousers, she flushed again, but picked them up bravely and plunged in like a little man; alas, the garment had been cut for a big one, and she found herself floundering in cloth that dangled at length over each foot. It was unfortunate that she should have caught sight of her figure reflected in a looking-glass at that moment; Miss Etty had to struggle with an inclination to cry in consequence. At last by sitting on the floor she found that she was able to turn the ends of the trousers up to her knees, and when she rose to her feet again the deed was accomplished. With one glance of fearful fascination at the mirror, Miss Etty hurried her riding-skirt over the horrid sight.

When she walked out into the store afterwards, and bought corn-meal at the counter, there was no sign of disturbance in her face, and in figure she only seemed a little stouter and taller. The store-keeper followed her to the horse-block, and lifted her bodily to the saddle; as he settled the stirrup, he looked up admiringly.

"If that don't beat all!" he whispered; "and you no bigger than my thumb, either!"

Although Rivertown was presumably well sentried by Federal troops, little Miss Etty Trot never had any difficulty in going in and out. She stopped now, as usual, to chat with the sentry; but this time he caught at her bridle, with a laugh.

"'Pears to me you set higher than when you came in," he said.

She knew him too well to be much frightened, and made no attempt to ride on; she even looked down at him and laughed also.

With a good-natured wink the man released the horse, and moved aside. Dick screamed with laughter when Miss Etty explained that she had winked back to keep him in a good humour.

"But the uniform, Miss Etty dear!—the brand-new uniform!" cried the delighted soldier. "I was thinking I should have to go clothed in my virtue. How did you get that through?"

To this he could get no answer; Miss Etty blushed and hung her head, but kept her secret.

Much sooner than either of them expected the uniform was to be worn. When McCulloch glanced through the papers Miss Etty handed over to him, he started to his feet, exclaimed aloud in his excitement, and rushed off to the depleted stables to order that the best horse left should be saddled immediately.

In the hurry of his departure Miss Etty had no time for questions; but as she ran out into the road and stood by his stirrup, he bent down for a last word and a half explanation.

She caught the words, "General Lee," "urgency," and "news of greatest importance." Then in the midst of her pleading reminder of his just-healed wound he was gone.

Within an hour he had returned to her, as has been told, on foot, hunted, all but taken.

When he recovered consciousness, his faithful nurse was sitting by his bedside, dropping hot tears on the twitching hand she held in hers.

"Miss Etty —"

"Oh, hush, my dear! I have sent Dan for the doctor; you must not try to speak."

"But I must — General Lee — the papers —"

He motioned impatiently toward the stimulant which she had been giving him, and after taking it he spoke more strongly.

"My horse was shot under me. I managed to hide the papers under a stone. Miss Etty —"

She bent her ear close to his lips. As she listened to his whispers, her face grew graver and graver.

"You see, the general must know," said the young man, feverishly.

"Yes."

"The doctor is loyal; he can take the message. Will he never come?"

"You forget how old the doctor is, Dick. It is forty miles to ride, and over the mountain."

"But the general must know."

"Yes, the general must know. My dear, my dear, how can I leave you!"

Dick struggled up on his elbow. "You — you — would you dare?"

"Hush! You must let me think. You will be needing me every moment."

He fell back in his bed and watched her with wonder; she was already kneeling, and like a little child she folded her hands together.

"O Lord, direct me; for I have lost my way," he heard her murmur.

"Amen," McCulloch whispered.

After a pause he spoke again, "The woods are always thickest and darkest where the light begins, Miss Etty."

The little figure rose, pathetically tiny even when standing. She bent over him, and kissed his forehead.

"Good-by, my dear," she said simply.

When Dan arrived with the old doctor, the cook was in the sick-room, and the only one who could have explained Miss Etty's disappearance was wild and incoherent with fever.

The hot sun went down in the heavens, and the edge of the white moon came up; from her horse's back Miss Etty watched the setting and rising.

"It must be hard never to see the end of anything," she thought. "Now, the sun will never know if I reach General Lee, unless the moon tells him."

She would not think serious thoughts; she did not dare. Putting them resolutely aside, Miss Etty had gone back in memory to the days before these troubles came. Trivial things lived vividly in her memory; she was a child once more, playing with her brother, swinging in grape-vine swings, and hunting water-snakes on the river-bank,—especially the wily serpent which always escaped them. When at last a chance blow from her stick killed it, she had cried inconsolably, and could only explain that she did n't know she loved it.

At this reflection Miss Etty laughed aloud, and started. The child became Miss Etty Trot again on a mission of life or death to many.

The dark hours before the moon came up had not been so hard to bear as these with ghostly shadows cast upon the road. In this mysterious light, her imagination roused, she saw a man in every tree and stump; before each bend of the road she lived through a capture, and turned every fence-corner with a heart which beat to suffocation.

An ever-present consciousness of the sick-room left behind came also, and stayed, — an undercurrent of trouble. Yet steadily on in the dim light, led by her tremulous bravery, the little woman rode over mountain, valley, and river to her general's camp.

"A lady to see General Lee at this hour of night! Impossible!"

It was the aide speaking sharply to a soldier standing at the entrance of the general's tent.

The man explained that she would give her message to no one else.

"Then tell her she must wait until morning."

A voice came from inside. "Bring her here to me," it said.

The soldier saluted the voice and departed into the darkness as he had come. The aide went back into the tent and, his eyes heavy with sleep, sat down by the table where General Lee was writing.

At a challenge from the sentry, he rose and held back the canvas flap; through the opening, Miss Etty Trot entered, looking almost a child in her close-fitting riding-habit.

General Lee raised his head and looked at her with extreme surprise; then rising quickly, he crossed the floor to meet her.

"What can I do for you?" he asked kindly.

With no preamble, Miss Etty lifted her face, and in low tones told the story she had come to tell. Her hair, loosened by her long ride, fell in little curling tendrils. A soft flush spread over her delicate features, her breath came quickly; but she stood with the quiet of high breeding, and spoke simply. General Grant was to cross the river the next day, with the intention of surprising the army.

The grave importance of her news was reflected in General Lee's face, as he bent his noble head lower and lower toward her, listening with rapt attention.

To the artistic eye of the young officer, standing in the background, he seemed the embodiment of thoughtful strength, and she of eager enthusiasm. The peculiar sweetness of her high voice, even in its whispers, caught his ear; and his admiration for the two contrasting figures, standing out against the white wall, deepened as he grasped their meaning better.

Picking up an old envelope, he pencilled a hasty sketch on its back. Beneath it, with the enthusiasm of a sad prescience, he wrote: "How the Confederacy held out so long." This scrap of paper is still among his most cherished possessions.

After Miss Etty had delivered her message, and answered a few pertinent questions, she knew that her work was done; and there being no further need of heroism, it took flight, leaving her trembling. General Lee's quick eye noted this.

"And you have ridden forty miles by night to tell me this!" he said.

The personal question confused Miss Etty, while veneration for the speaker overwhelmed her. As she faltered out an answer, a smile of exquisite enjoyment passed over the face of the general's aide. His commander's countenance remained immovable, and the little lady never knew that she had said "yes, ma'am," to the great soldier. His next question was even more kindly and gentle.

"My dear child, how could your father let you go?"

"I am thirty-three. My father is dead, and there was no one else."

There was something infinitely touching about her as she stood tremulously asserting her loneliness.

General Lee's manner of gentle deference, his generous appreciation of the service she had rendered, failed to reassure her. She was still flushed and trembling when, with his words of grave praise and farewell still ringing in her ears, she left the tent in the escort of the aide, quarters having been hastily arranged for her in a crowded farmhouse close by.

But despite Miss Etty's awe, her eyes had noted a brass button which lay upon the half-written page on the table, and they had fastened upon it hungrily more than once, not unobserved by the younger officer. As he bade her good-night at the farmhouse, he laid something hard and round in her hand; when she could examine it, she found it was the coveted brass button.

Miss Etty fell asleep that night like a happy child, with the bit of metal clasped close in her hand; and when she awoke deep in the next day, the great army was gone.

Then, although her hospitable host made every effort to detain her, she would not rest longer. Her duties were taken as they came, and Dick was next in order.

Poor Dick! Dan met his mistress at the door of the Peninsula House, dolefully shaking his head.

"He 's boun' ter go, honey," he said with unctuous enjoyment of woe.

Miss Etty ran up the stair, straight from her horse's back to Dick's bedside. With the first glance at his face, her heart sank. He looked at her with vague, unseeing eyes; even her voice failed to rouse him.

Her own weariness and long journey were forgotten. She left the sick-room only to change her riding-habit for her usual home gown, and to fasten General Lee's button in the button-hole at her throat. Again and again through the long watches of that night, she gained courage from the touch of the hard metal against her soft chin.

"I am thankful I sewed it there," she thought; "I should never have been able to touch it, with my hands so busy."

They were full to overflowing, for she had many parts to play. Dick did not know her as "Miss Etty." First she was "mother," and in that character a perfected actress; in her soothing touch and voice, he missed nothing that he called for. It was less easy to be "John," and to listen calmly to broken stories of flood and field, of home and boy life. But it was almost unbearable to her when she became "Alice." Dick called out against her as heartless, faithless; and it hurt her unreasonably.

When he caught her hands and covered them with passionate kisses, pouring out burning words, the primitive little maiden-lady shrank and shrivelled. She was frightened and bewildered beyond measure under this delirious wooing; but she stood bravely at her post, and at last he knew her.

"Is it you? Does the general know? Were you in time?"

"Yes, the general knows, Dick. I was in time. The army is safe." She vainly tried to steady her voice.

At its tremulous note, McCulloch looked up and read his fate in her face as in an open book.

He closed his eyes and lay so still that Miss Etty thought him unconscious; but as she bent over him, with the fictitious strength of fever, he took her hand and drew a seal-ring from his finger, fitting it on hers. The significance of his action almost broke her heart.

"Ah, no, no!" she began, sobbing; but he stopped her with the ghost of his old smile.

"Don't, Miss Etty dear; did you think I should be afraid?"

And then he began to ramble again, wandering among the places of this world, strange to his nurse, and a little later, among the many mansions of another, strange to us all.

Miss Etty was once more left alone in the old Peninsula House.

Twelve years had gone by since the day Richard McCulloch's mother received two letters which had struggled through the lines together. One was from Dick, telling of his wound and illness, and dwelling with affectionate humour on his quaint little nurse. The second bore a later date, and was signed "Henrietta Trot."

From this letter the mother learned that her son would never return. "We have laid his mortal remains in the southern corner of our graveyard, dressed in the uniform he wore in life, and looking toward the country he loved and died to save," wrote Miss Etty, in her somewhat old-fashioned phrases.

The great wave of war sweeping over the country had washed away Mrs. McCulloch's patrimony as a house of cards; it was not in her power to fulfil the wish of her heart that her son's body should lie in the graveyard of his native town among his brother-soldiers.

Like thousands of her Southern sisters, who resentfully survived the wreck, she struggled on, widowed, childless, with but one hope and aim in the world. For this end she worked with feverish energy; for this she stinted herself in food and raiment.

One night, when almost twelve years had passed, her hope seemed incredibly near a certainty. She sat in her sparely furnished room, in front of the table on which was spread neatly assorted piles of clean bank-notes.

"Two hundred and seventy-five," she counted, — "two hundred and eighty, ninety," — her voice trembled, — "ninety-two, ninety-seven."

She opened her reticule, took from it three one-dollar bills, and laid them with the rest. "Three hundred dollars," whispered the woman who had spent that sum on a single gown in a past now almost incredible, — "three hundred dollars," she repeated in an awe-struck murmur, and then burst into tears. Some of the warm drops fell on the bank-notes; she wiped them jealously away with her handkerchief. "You are to bring me back my boy," she said, fingering the notes tenderly.

The sum she had set herself to earn and save had fluctuated in her keeping. Sometimes a season of little work had obliged her to draw upon it, sometimes illness had diminished the hoard; but now it was all there, and she gloated over it. She had trusted her treasure to no bank, to no other keeping than her own.

She sat thinking intently, for now she could go no further without help; to whom could she confide this sacred trust?

Mrs. McCulloch ran over in her mind the list of names of those friends whose proffered aid she had hitherto proudly refused, deliberately choosing her grief as her stern and sole companion.

At last she settled on Colonel John Bassett; he had been her son's friend, and General Lee's aide, — what better credentials could one ask? She slept that night with the price of her boy's home-coming beneath her pillow, and the first thing in the morning sought Colonel Bassett's office with the precious package in her hand.

Although the brave soldier was now the busy lawyer, he laid by his work instantly on her entrance, receiving her with cordial greeting; and when she told him the purpose of her visit, his eyes filled with sudden tears.

His old comrade's mother had rejected every offer of material assistance; had he but chanced to think of it, here was something he might have done years ago. As he looked at her worn, triumphant face and joy-lit eyes, at the hardly-earned money, — contrasting it with his own comparatively easily made hundreds, — Colonel Bassett bent quickly forward and gathered her hands into his.

"My dear old friend, let me—" was on his lips, but a finer instinct withheld him; he drew back, folded the money together, and locked it in his safe. "I will see to it all personally," he said; "you may take all care in this matter from off your heart."

When Mrs. McCulloch gave Colonel Bassett Miss Etty's letter, he repeated the signature aloud, thoughtfully.

"Henrietta Trot," he said, "I have surely heard that name before. Henrietta Trot—no, I don't place it. The directions are clear, however, and the grave will be easy to find. You may trust all to me, Mrs. McCulloch;" and with a heart softened by grateful tears, Mrs. McCulloch left the office.

On the day of Richard McCulloch's reinterment, all the town, in carriages and on foot, followed the hearse and its military escort to the cemetery. Those who did not know the details of the mother's sacrifice, guessed them, and wished to pay respect to the brave son, and perhaps braver mother.

Mrs. McCulloch, leaning on Colonel Bassett's arm, stood close to the open grave, shedding not unhappy tears. She could hear the wailing melody of the funeral march, and see the dear defeated banner waving above her.

"Dust to dust, ashes to ashes."

The remnant of Dick's regiment drew up,—some of its individual members mere remnants themselves,—and three volleys of musketry fired over the grave finished the solemn ceremony.

When Colonel Bassett handed the remainder of Mrs. McCulloch's money to her, it was a sum so much larger than she had expected, that she exclaimed in surprise,—

"Why, there is enough left to pay for the monument,

and have everything just as I longed to see it!" she said, flushing with pleasure. "But, Colonel Bassett, are you quite sure that I owe nothing more? Have I paid everything?"

"I have settled every bill, I assure you," he answered, and had the reward of seeing the anxious question which had risen in her eyes fade away.

"She is a changed woman," thought Colonel Bassett, when the monument was at last in place, and he watched Mrs. McCulloch bending lovingly over the grave, — "she is a changed woman. Those poor bones and that cold marble have softened her as a flesh and blood child might. Better so, perhaps; those cannot be taken from her."

Yet the next morning's mail brought him the following letter, —

COL. JOHN BASSETT:

SIR, — I demand that you at once return the body of my sister, Miss Etty Trot, which you stole from our family graveyard two weeks ago. I understand that you identified it as the body of one Richard McCulloch by a seal ring and a Confederate button. The ring was given to my sister by said Richard McCulloch on his death-bed, and the button was a gift from General Lee. Both mementos were buried with her by her request. Expecting immediate restitution on your part. Truly,

S. V. L. C. TROT

"Trot, — Miss Etty Trot," repeated Colonel Bassett; "that was the name. General Lee's button, — I gave it to her myself."

It was all coming back to him now, dropping down from some shelf in his memory where it had lain hidden. He took up an old portfolio, and from among its contents, selected a packet, on the back of which was written, "Sketches of General Lee."

He turned them over gently, as men finger treasures, and drew out one which he laid on the table before him. It was evidently a hasty drawing, made on the back of an old envelope; but it was a vivid reproduction of the meeting between Miss Etty and General Lee, which he had witnessed when the general's aide.

"There she is," he exclaimed triumphantly. There are some people who, although seen but once and then perhaps briefly, have yet the power to touch a chord in our hearts which vibrates to-morrow, or even twelve years after, as to-day.

Colonel Bassett looked affectionately at the drawing of the tiny figure.

"And so it is you we have buried with military honours. Bless your poor little bones!" he said, laughing. "Well, no man deserved it better."

He thought of the men of the dead regiment she lay among, and of the monument over the gentle little lady, which spoke of "war's alarms" and a "hero dead," and laughed aloud, thinking how Dick himself would have enjoyed the joke. Then he suddenly remembered Dick's mother, and his laughter ended abruptly. What was this going to mean to her?

What it meant to Colonel Bassett was a trip to the Peninsula House by the next train.

On his arrival there, he found Mr. S. V. L. C. Trot established in the house of his fathers after fifteen years' absence.

A weakling in intellect and morals, he was dominated by the old slave Dan, who, ever since Miss Etty's death, had been seeking this degenerate son, and had now brought him home to reign over rack and ruin.

Dan was old and bent and hideous, with a face like an ape. It was on him that the weight of testimony fell. He had buried Richard McCulloch, and his mistress had read the funeral service, which was more than many of the dead received in those troublous days.

"An' you did n't have no right to come a-gobblin' up our bones," he growled to Colonel Bassett.

But Colonel Bassett would not be antagonized. He explained patiently that he would willingly have asked permission, had any one been there to give it; but he found the homestead deserted and rank with weeds. The body was lying in the southern corner, as described in the letter, and he had supposed that all was correct.

Dan led Colonel Bassett out to the graveyard, and illustrated the story on the spot.

"Miss Etty, she got it inter her hade dat dar warnt room fur but one grave in dis corner. I knowed better. Dar warnt no use in ways'in' good groun,' nor in talkin' to her, nuther, when she got sot. I jes' *eased* it along in de diggin'. Miss Etty, she rared 'bout it; but 't warnt no use when de diggin' was done. Dar war room fur anoder grave, too; fur I buried *her* dar. I knowed; but then she warnt but a scrap."

It was too plainly true; the only question that remained was how to deal with the facts.

Colonel Bassett looked at the vacuous face of the shiftless owner of the Peninsula, who was sitting on the top of the graveyard fence, with his feet hooked in the lower rail.

He hesitated; but then the memory of Mrs. McCulloch's face, with its newly-come peace softening it, rose before him.

"It will be but a pious fraud, after all," he thought; yet he spoke with an effort.

"May I discuss this matter alone with you, Mr. Trot?" he asked; and Mr. Trot, unwinding his feet from the fence-rail, assented.

They walked to the house, leaving Dan swelling with outraged dignity.

What that interview cost Colonel Bassett's fine sense of honour, no one but himself will ever know; what it cost his pocket, is a secret which Mr. S. V. L. C. Trot shares with him.

When Dan would have again opened the question of the graves, his so-called master, with new-born arrogance, bade him hold his tongue, — the matter had been settled between Colonel Bassett and himself.

The old man stood silent, peering at him from the corners of his blear eyes.

"Hit 's loose change, dang it!" he muttered to himself, as he turned away. "He shell go on a spree to-morrow. Dar won't be no livin' wid him tell he gits rid on it all."

On Decoration Day the south branch of the Potomac ran brawling and quarrelling about the Peninsula, as usual. By the point of land where the graveyard stood, a rock rose out of the water; the waves splashed and foamed against it, leaping high, as if striving to reach the top, and from there look over into the yard, where six feet of earth seemed to have burst into bloom in a day, with rare exotic blossoms, all red and white. Old Dan's ape-like face bent over them, and his black hands were placing the flowers.

"Cunnel Bassett 's fur a-smoothin' him down wid dese, is he?" he muttered contemptuously. "Miss Etty, she have dickered him outen his buryin' do." He laughed with a little crowing chuckle, and stooped to touch a glowing leaf with his horny forefinger; perhaps a sense of tardy justice smote him, for he added, slowly, —

"He warnt half bad, nuther, he warnt. I reckon ef she likes hit, he ain't begrutchin' none on it to her."

FIFTEEN COUNTY ROCK.

Fifteen County Rock.

HOW the Rock came to be there on the mountain-side, it never quite knew. It held a vague memory of an intense cold; of being swept powerfully along with masses of snow and ice,—a horrible grinding, groaning, and crushing; after that, stillness for years and years.

It was a long time before the great boulder even learned to separate night and day. Rocks think slowly. The sun beat down and warmed it through and through to the very heart; the soft mist and dampness wrapped it by night; and gradually it grew to know and love them all,—but always loving most the moist, clinging clouds that come by night or by day.

From the mountain-side the boulder looked down over what is now called fifteen counties. There, majestic rivers marched grandly, and tiny streams, threading the land, sought the rivers. These were the life-giving arteries and veins, and by reason of their being the country smiled.

Hundreds of years passed, and a deeper and deeper contentment settled down upon the Rock; then it was discovered.

But long before men discovered the boulder, the boulder discovered men. It had watched in the distance their building of houses and mills, their herding of cattle and ploughing of fields, and yet made no attempt to intrude. But after men discovered the Rock, they were always climbing up from the plain below to stand on its back and see what it had been looking at for hundreds of years.

Fifteen County Rock, as they called it, did not then know how to laugh; but it learned this after listening to a man who stood on its broad back and pointed out an ant's nest to a child. He was laughing at the tiny workers as he described the division of labour among them, — some hurrying here and some there. Then it was that the Rock laughed to itself gently, remembering how human beings had seemed when looked down upon from above.

Fifteen County Rock began to hear many strange things now; but nothing stirred it from its deep contentment until one autumn day something very strange happened. The sun had risen warm, but the air was cool and crisp with the chill of the night still in it; everything seemed to be alive and happy. A little field on the mountain-side laughed aloud when the breeze passed over it. Each small blade of grass stirred and twinkled, and the tall ones bent double with mirth. There was no warning that anything unusual was to occur; so the Rock paid small attention when a young man came out of the wood and mounted to its topmost ridge.

"Ah!" he cried, as he looked down; then he added softly, "what hath God wrought?"

He stood for a long time motionless, looking over the land; then he took out paper and pencil and sat down to sketch.

Presently a great black dog ran out from the bushes, leaping about him with short barks.

"Down, Matt!" called the man; and the dog lay quiet with his head on the ground, but managed gradually to crawl on his belly to his master's side and lay his head on his master's foot.

The man looked down. "You old goose!" he said, laughing.

He rubbed the dog's head with the end of his pencil as he spoke, and turned the sketch toward him.

"Do you know what that is? It is a picture, and for your rival, sir; I shall bring her here herself some day."

He looked dreamily out at the scene below him, until the dog sat up and recalled his attention by striking him on the knee with his awkward paw.

His master bent and took the shaggy head between his hands, while the creature gazed up into his face with eyes which were like a gentle woman's.

"Matt, Matt, why have n't you a soul?" said the man; "but perhaps you may have one after all; I sometimes think so. If you have, look!"

He caught the dog's collar, led him to the edge of the Rock, and pointed below. But the dog only beat his tail on the ground and looked down uneasily; then at some sound in the bushes, he slobbered, broke away, and ran off.

"Matt is surely of the beasts that perish," said the man; and there was disappointment in his voice. He finished his sketch hastily, and then went back into the wood, whistling on his way.

"A soul!" thought the Rock. "What is a soul?"

This was the first time that it had ever heard of such a thing, and it grew curious and longed to know more; but though it listened and listened, of the many who climbed up the mountain, none talked of souls.

At last came a party of young girls with little hammers in their hands, and bags swinging by their sides. An elderly man was with them, who talked long and earnestly.

"Glacial striations, marginal moraines, roches moutonnees," was what he spoke of, while the Rock listened patiently, though it understood nothing.

Finally, the word it had been waiting so long to hear, was used.

"I am sometimes led to believe that there exists, even in rock and stone, a species of soul, of being, a — a —"

"An innate soul, Professor?" asked the prettiest of the young girls.

"Yes, yes, exactly; that was good, good, very good."

When the professor left, the girls crowded about the pretty one who had spoken.

"What did you mean?" they asked. "We did not understand. What is an innate soul?"

The Rock waited with deep anxiety for her answer.

She broke into a peal of laughter. "I have not an idea," she cried.

Then they all laughed their careless gay laughter.

"The professor knew," thought Fifteen County Rock, in its disappointment. "It may be that I have a soul."

Twice in that same day did it hear the word. An old man in clerical dress and with long white hair climbed stiffly up its rough side; he shaded his eyes with his hand, and looked out at the setting sun from under his bushy white eyebrows.

"My soul doth magnify the Lord," he said over and over again.

There was a young man with him who listened and said nothing.

Presently a party of tourists came, — men and women, — chattering and laughing. Some looked at the sunset, and some at each other.

One of the women, no longer very young, but in youthful dress, busied herself in collecting the scraps of paper and bits of egg-shell left by a former picnic-party; she hid them all under a stone, announcing to one and another in a high nasal voice, "The face of Nature, you know, — defending the face of Nature."

The old clergyman watched her with interest, and catching his eye, she paused a moment.

"Don't you think, sir, that a sunset like this *adds?*" she asked, waving a brisk hand toward the horizon.

"It adds, Madam, most certainly," he replied gravely.

She walked away with her satisfied, jaunty little step, leaving the young man shaking with laughter.

"A genuine New England clam," he whispered.

The old clergyman's blue eyes twinkled under the pent-house of his shaggy brows. "Let her alone," he said; "even clams have a soul hid away somewhere. You may think that remark *shoppy* now, young man; but when you are as old as I am, you will know it is only truth."

"What can this *soul* be?" thought the Rock, uneasily. "If even clams have souls, why not I?"

But the days went by, and though it learned many things from the people who came and went, and who talked on many subjects, it heard nothing more of souls; so a little gnawing speck of discontent grew and almost ate away the great contentment which had possessed it of old.

One evening, when the sunlight had no more warmth of colour, and was only a pale golden tint in the air and a reflection on the clouds which lay softly pillowed against each other in the west, a great black dog ran out of the bushes and on to the back of the Rock. With a thrill that struck to its very centre, it recognized Matt.

"His master will follow, and then,—then perhaps, I shall know."

Very soon Matt's master appeared; but he came slowly, for he was not alone. There was a woman with him, and he was helping her to climb; she was exceedingly beautiful,—more beautiful than any one the Rock had ever seen. Before they reached the summit, she sat down on a stone, breathing quickly.

"It is so steep and warm," she said, smiling. "You have chosen a poor comrade, I fear."

The man took off his straw hat and fanned her, with a reply at which she smiled again, and laid her hand on his shoulder with a light, caressing gesture.

"You will spoil me," she answered, and turned her shapely throat to catch the waves of air. "Have we much farther to go?"

"No; but a little way. I want to show you the very spot where I made the sketch for you. Are you quite sure that you are rested now? Then come."

He helped her to the top of the Rock, and led her to the edge. "Look!" he cried exultingly, and pointed below.

She opened her great serious eyes widely, and looked over toward the west; they were brown eyes, that reminded Fifteen County Rock of the stags which had come to stand on its back in the years before it was discovered.

The two stood hand in hand, silent. The man looked at the sunset and then at his companion.

"Love," she said, at last, and her voice was very musical, "do you see that charming pink and pearl cloud? It would exactly suit my colouring in a gown."

The black dog brushed against his master, and he stooped to caress him. As he did so, he dropped the hand he had been holding. He took the dog's head in his hands, as he had once before, and looked down into the dumb creature's beautiful eyes with a curious smile.

"Matt, I told you on this Rock, last year, that you had no soul. Well, old boy, I take it all back; you may have a soul, for aught I know to the contrary."

The woman turned her lovely head. "Don't you think, dear, that it may be irreverent to talk of souls in that way?"

"Perhaps— If you are ready, we will go now," he answered gently.

In the quiet which followed their going, Fifteen County Rock laughed again and again at itself and its own folly. For a year it had been striving to learn what a soul meant from beings who did not themselves know; but it had learned a better lesson.

"Nothing shall ever again move me from my deep contentment," thought Fifteen County Rock, humbly.

A LEGACY.

A LEGACY.

HALF on the bank of the Swanton River, and half on the bay which leads Swanton to the sea, stands the town of Ayre. It is a quaint, straggling little township, growing, apparently, with no prenatal arrangement of streets and avenues. Where one had been minded to buy land and build a home, it would seem to have been done with no interference; the result was picturesque in the extreme, and not very uncomfortable. When a street stretched out too long, it was pierced by queer, narrow courts which gave an air of mystery to the most innocent spot on earth. That carriages must drive around these blocks was a small matter where only four families owned carriages; and besides, what need was there for haste?

The population of Ayre consisted chiefly of women and children, — the men having gone forth to war in larger spheres. Artists and oystermen were the only workmen who came there, to seek material for the vocations they followed. Swanton was renowned for its oysters, and bits of the drowsy beauty of the little town hung on many a studio wall.

On an exquisite summer noon Anthony Alderdyce, one of the first-named wandering brotherhood, sat painting in a glade on the side of one of the cool, wooded hills which rise on that bank of the river known to Ayre as "t'other side Swanton." In figure he was rather thickset, of medium height, and particularly well developed about the chest and shoulders. As he bent over the canvas, his face showed massive, almost to heaviness; but when he glanced up, the eager expression of a pair of fine, thoughtful eyes counteracted the immobility of the other features. Something in face and figure gave an impression of belonging to a past and more stately generation when a stock and laces and powdered hair were in vogue.

He was an ardent disciple, and painted with an absorbed rapidity, though so quietly that a tiny chipmunk ran with fearless security in and out of its home in an old log close by.

Suddenly a woman's startled cry rang through the woods.

The little chipmunk flew scurrying to its hole, and Alderdyce started to his feet, dropping his brush from his hand; it was charged with dark paint, and in falling, struck the picture, leaving an ugly black line.

On the crest of the hill behind lurked a bog, formed by the summer rains held in a ridge of the ground. It was from this direction that the cry had come; and as Alderdyce turned, he saw a young girl struggling helplessly in the soft mould, where she had sunk to her ankles.

He ran forward, calling out to her, somewhat sharply, to stand quiet; and when he reached the bog's edge she was standing obediently motionless, but with so hopeless an expression of despair on her face that Alderdyce, knowing her position to be more ludicrous than dangerous, almost laughed aloud.

While assuring her that he would soon extricate her, he reviewed the situation, and saw that it would be quicker work to reach her from the side where he stood than to round the bog. He threw brushwood on the treacherous ground, and walking on it carefully, stretched out his hand.

"Can you reach it?" he asked. "Gently! or we shall both plunge in and leave no one to come to the rescue."

The girl grasped his fingers tightly, and he cautiously worked his hand down to her wrist, and then to her arm.

"Now, steady!" he cried; and with a sudden wrench drew her toward him, caught her quickly before the frail brush broke under the double burden, and dragged her to dry land. "That was not badly done, I flatter myself," he said, laughingly, as he released her.

But the girl stepped back, and looked at him with wide, frightened eyes; her cheeks were crimson, and her quick breathing told how her heart was fluttering.

Her figure, though immature, was full of graceful suggestions, and her face, in spite of its frightened expression, was extremely beautiful; above its oval rose a cloud of warm brown hair, which was gathered together at the back of her daintily poised head, and there pierced by a slender, venomous-looking dagger with a jewelled hilt. The rich, barbaric ornament contrasted oddly with the softness of her hazel eyes and the gentleness of her expression; but it gave a most piquant touch to her beauty, Alderdyce thought, as he looked curiously at her.

It was plain that he had thoroughly startled her.

"I trust that I have not hurt you," he said apologetically; "there was no other way."

In a timid voice, and evidently by a great effort, she spoke for the first time. There was a decided though not unpleasant accent in her English.

"You have been very kind," she began, then paused, and blushing painfully, faltered something which Alderdyce could not understand.

"What is it?" he asked, bending forward and speaking gently, fearing each moment that she would fly off as shyly as the little chipmunk.

"My — my shoes —"

Alderdyce looked down and saw that she was standing in stockinged feet, her shoes left in the bog. After a search he found them, the ribboned bow of one and the pointed toe of the other sticking up pathetically from the black mud. By the aid of a long stick, he was able to dig them out, each a shapeless lump.

"Will you acknowledge these?" he asked, holding them up.

But their owner came forward with eagerness, and took them daintily between finger and thumb.

"Thank you," she murmured; "you have been very kind to me."

Alderdyce, fearful of startling her by offers of further assistance, stood looking on in wondering amusement.

A bough of one of the neighbouring trees grew downward by some freak, then out and up again; and the girl seated herself on this leafy swing as naturally as a wood-nymph might, and began a careful cleaning of one of her shoes with a small stick.

Who was she, and whence had she come? That she was not a native of Ayre, Alderdyce felt assured; and he placed her as a daughter of the South by her warm colouring and soft accent.

Although apparently absorbed in her work, he knew that his presence was not forgotten, as the very sweep of her eye-lashes betrayed consciousness. He sat down on an opposite stone in silence as unbroken as her own, and taking up the second boot, began to clean it in the same manner.

That a struggle of some kind was going on in the mind of his companion, was presently evident by her expression.

Alderdyce saw her eyelids flutter slowly up, and considerately, and with some wiliness, dropped his own. At last the young girl laid down both stick and shoe, and folding her hands, spoke ceremoniously, if a little gaspingly, —

"My name is Conchita Maria de Santillana, and I live with my father in Ayre; but we are of Spain."

The effort made, she relapsed into sudden silence again.

Alderdyce, with an equally courteous ceremony, laid down his stick and shoe also, and lifted his hat, bowing gravely.

"Thank you. My name is Anthony Alderdyce; I am an artist, and I have just come to Ayre."

There was nothing in his face or voice to betray how infinitely amusing he found the stately comedy; and his eyes, which he knew too well to trust, were guarded by their lids.

But when he looked up the next moment, surprise had driven all other expression from them.

"An artist," Conchita Santillana had cried, clasping her hands, — "an artist! Ah, how glad I am!"

"Are you of the brotherhood, then?"

"No; but my father is, and his greatest pleasure is to be with artists."

"And has he not taught you?"

"Only a little; but I can look at a painting and think: Would my father like it?—and if I decide not, then it is sure to be poor."

"You can always tell then?"

"Always. Is that strange?"

Alderdyce, conscious that he was walking on ground not much surer than the neighbouring bog, went on, feeling his way cautiously.

"I was painting when I heard your cry," he said, carelessly glancing toward his easel.

As Conchita turned and saw the easel standing on the hillside, the last vestige of her shyness vanished.

"Oh, may I see it when I have cleaned my boot?" she asked. "Why, yours is almost done."

"Let me finish yours too, then; give it to me, and look at the picture now, if you will."

Conchita sprang up and walked quickly away over the soft grass of the glade. Alderdyce smiled again as he looked after her, struck by the easy unconcern she showed of her unconventionally garbed feet.

When he joined her, she was kneeling in front of his picture and looked up to greet him approvingly.

"You spoke truly; you are an artist."

The successful, petted young painter stooped suddenly, apparently to pick up his colour-box.

"How my father will like this!" the girl went on, looking lovingly herself at the spirited sketch. "You will let him see it, will you not?"

"You like it, then?" said Alderdyce.

"No," she answered, looking at him reproachfully; "I don't *like* paintings, I *feel* them."

"I beg your pardon," replied the artist, humbly, and turning away again to collect his brushes.

Artists and scientists complain that, in painting and experiments, the novice will fasten on the most unimportant accidents to dwell on; and Alderdyce observed, with approval, that his new critic made no reference to the dark blot on the canvas until the beauties of the painting had been absorbed; then she only pointed to it and looked up inquiringly.

"That marks your entrance," Alderdyce explained; "I dropped my brush there when you screamed."

"Have I spoiled your picture?" she asked, distressed.

"No, no; I can work it in somehow."

"But how?"

"Well, for instance, that dark spot is not unlike your gown; the picture is only improved if you will come into it in reality. Will you?"

"It seems but just."

"Have you ever been a model before? Do you know how tedious it is?"

"Oh, I am always a model; more than I am myself, I think. I am a better Madonna than anything else; my father calls my Madonna expression perfect."

"May I see your Madonna expression?"

"Surely, if you wish."

She lifted her head and raised her soft eyes to heaven, while an expression of exquisite meekness and resignation grew on her features.

With dismay, Alderdyce found himself laughing aloud at last, despite his fear that she would disappear into the wood from which she came; the metamorphosis, so sudden and unexpected, proved too much for his self-control.

But to his relief, the Madonna only became Conchita again, and looked wounded.

"You do not like it, then?"

"On the contrary," returned Alderdyce, hastily, still choking a little, "it was beautiful; but how do you manage it?"

"I learned it in the mirror, and it took a long time; are you sure that you like it?"

"No; I don't *like* Madonnas, — I *feel* them."

Conchita, turning quickly toward him, looked up suspiciously into his grave face. Although his eyes met hers in all outward innocence, she suddenly detected the quizzical gleam lurking in them, and responded to it by a merry laugh which broke the last barrier.

"And are you really willing to sit for me?" asked Alderdyce again; "after seeing how you can pose, I am hungry to begin."

"I think I surely owe it to you," she replied, glancing at the smeared canvas; "but do you think my father could object?"

The temptation was great; the sunbeams filtering through the leaves fell on the girl's hair, played on the soft oval of her cheek, and lit up the jewels in the dagger's hilt. "Would a sane parent permit her to wander about wearing a costly bauble like that?" thought Alderdyce.

Conchita was awaiting his answer; and as she turned her head one of the tiny rays of motey light fell flickeringly on the hollow of her throat. Surely men's fortunes do hang on a balance as fine as a hair when a mote in the sunbeam can turn the scale.

"Your father could not object," said Alderdyce, decidedly. "Come, we must not lose a moment of this light; you can stand on these boards while your boots dry."

The painting began, and with its progress the artist grew more and more absorbed in his subject. The afternoon sun shot through an opening in the trees and lay in a long line on the grass which floored the glade; Alderdyce painted the graceful figure as if walking unconsciously forward in the warm colour of this sun-path, — and as he reproduced the lines of her figure and the beauty of her face its charm took possession of him. He soon found that she not only knew how to take a pose, but how to hold it, and the familiarity of her part as a model seemed to open her heart. Alderdyce, who was painting against time, knew all that there was to be known of her everyday life with her father, her work and her play, before the lengthening shadows warned him of the coming dusk. The existence she told of seemed to him pitifully cabined for both.

"Can you not remember your home in Spain?" he asked, hoping to gain some knowledge of her life there.

But Conchita remembered very little. Her mother had died when she was quite a little child, she said, and her father found that he could not live where everything, even the air she had breathed, reminded him of her; so they came to America and to Ayre, — and that was all.

"But have you no companions, no friends?"

"No; none, really, — except my father."

"But your father, — has he none?"

"Oh, he has me; and now and then an artist who comes to Ayre, as you have."

"And you are contented? You never grow tired of each other?" asked Alderdyce, smiling.

"I don't know, — ought we? I never thought of it."

"Then don't think now," he answered, a little conscience-stricken. "There, the light has gone at last, and before I could really finish. I wonder if your shoes are dry yet."

"Where did you put them?"

"On a stone in the sun, hot enough to have roasted them long ago. You shall put them on, and then you may see your picture."

But when he brought her the shoes, it was with an expression of comical penitence and dismay on his face. Conchita gave a little cry of consternation when she saw them; the work of destruction so well begun by the bog, had been ably carried on by the hot sun above and the hot stone below. Bent, warped, twisted, the once dainty shoes were a caricature of the foot whose shape they had lately taken.

"You will only bruise your feet by trying to force those on them," Alderdyce expostulated; "pray don't attempt it."

But in spite of his remonstrance, she sat down on the grass, wrestling vainly with the impossible. At last she flung the wrecks from her in petulant despair.

"I have not only hurt my feet but my hands," she cried, aggrievedly looking at her reddened fingers.

"So much for kicking against the pricks, — I warned you, you know."

"But I had to try. How can I get home?"

"You can't, unless I take pity on you and manage it."

"Then will you take me home?" she asked, looking up with child-like confidence; "but how can you manage it?"

Alderdyce laughed as he looked down at the slight figure on the grass at his feet.

"If nothing else, I can carry you, you tiny thing!" he said lightly.

The moment he had spoken, he saw his mistake. The girl's open face closed as a frosted flower; her eyes darkened and dilated.

"I can walk quite easily," she said, rising; "and I must bid you good-evening now."

She turned from him and walked down the glade into the wood.

Alderdyce hesitated a moment, abusing his own stupidity, and then followed.

He was soon by her side, as after leaving the grass of the glade, her progress, with only thin stockings as a protection from wood-briers and stones, was necessarily slow. She did not attempt to ignore his presence as he at first thought she meant to do, but paused, turning her head with a stately, inquiring gesture. However awkward the position in which she placed him, the artist in Alderdyce applauded the action of her attitude, and the man in him its spirit.

"You are right to be offended," he said, "and I am ready to accept punishment; but pray let me assure you that I was stupid, not impertinent. Can you forgive me?"

"I don't think I can," she answered deliberately, "though I will try. Good-evening."

But the prospect of a remote reconciliation seemed not satisfactory to the offender, who still walked by her side, keeping pace with her uncertain steps.

Conchita trod on a brier, struck her foot against a

stone, stepped on another thorny plant, and then turned on Alderdyce with a flash in her eye, less discouraging to him than her former composure.

"Why do you follow me?" she asked.

"Because it is unsafe for you to go home alone; but if you prefer it, I will not speak to you."

She walked on, making no answer, and then stopped again suddenly. "The picture, — where is it?"

"On the easel."

"It will be ruined."

"Well, at least it will not try walking through the woods with bare feet."

"It will be ruined," she repeated.

"Very likely," answered Alderdyce, carelessly, and with a strategy which he felt shamelessly apparent.

"If you don't go back for it, I shall," cried Conchita, with indignant decision. "I saw both pigs and cows as I came up the hill; I won't have it left there alone."

"I am more than willing to go back for it if you will promise to wait for me here."

"Then I do promise."

Carefully hiding his exultation, Alderdyce left her sitting on the trunk of a felled tree, and went back to strap his picture and general impedimenta together. He picked up his favourite brushes, and looked at them with affection as they lay in his hand.

"You blessed little sables," he said, "I wonder if I could really have considered leaving you to pigs and cows. Well, not yet anyway."

When he rejoined Conchita, he brought with him two flat pieces of wood. "There are your new shoes," he said. "Will you try them on?"

She looked at him distrustfully. "How are they shoes?"

"Well, to be accurate, they are only sandals; but it is the best I can do. Will you try them on?"

"Y-yes."

"Then set your foot on this board, and let me mark the shape."

He knelt before her as disarmingly business-like as a shoemaker; and Conchita hesitatingly put out her pretty foot with its high instep and curved lines.

Alderdyce began to draw a line about it on the board, but stopped suddenly with an exclamation: "What have you done to yourself? Here is actual blood."

Conchita looked down anxiously to see a little red line trickling from a cut on the side of her foot.

"It was a sharp stone," she explained, changing colour. "I did not know it was bleeding, and I hate blood."

"Then don't look at it," said Alderdyce, "I can bind it up; it is not very bad."

Nor was it; but it served to startle Conchita into submission to his services, and she was visibly softened by the gentleness and care with which he bound the scratch, using strips torn from his own handkerchief as a bandage.

The surgical work finished, Alderdyce began whittling out the sandals. He had no better instrument than his penknife; but as he handled that national tool with the dexterity of the born American, the sandals were not without shape when he finished them.

"But how shall I keep them on?" asked Conchita, who sat watching, deeply interested.

"With latchets, of course; here they are."

He tore the remainder of his handkerchief into ribbons, which he bound into the wood, and then held up the completed work.

"Are they not superb works of art?" he asked.

She stretched out her hand with a laugh of delight, but Alderdyce drew back.

"No," he said; "I am a mercenary soul, I only work for pay. What will you give me for them?"

"What do you want?"

"Well, I have a corner on the market, you see; I can ask what I please."

"But I must have them, or I can't get home."

"Exactly; that's what I calculated on when I bought in all the sandal stock. These represent a *deal*. Do you know what that is?"

"No; but I do want the sandals."

"Then you must pay for them, and I hold them high." He dangled them before her as he spoke. "These must bring a full and free forgiveness, without a reservation. Is it a sale?"

"Yes," she answered, holding out an eager hand.

But Alderdyce flung the sandals into her lap, and took the outstretched hand in his. "Thank you," he said; "this ratifies the bargain."

When Conchita stood up in the rude makeshifts, she was laughing merrily again; and the journey home began with the old easy relations established between them.

"I have not seen my picture yet," she said; "but you will show it to me later, will you not?"

"You shall see it, of course."

"And my father, too? It would give him so much pleasure."

Alderdyce assented here also, although he had his doubts of the latter clause.

Clever as the sandals were, they were not shoes nor so easy to walk in. The progress through the woods, in the rapidly closing darkness, was slow; and slower still when the wood-path struck into an oyster-shell road which led to the bridge over Swanton. Just opposite Ayre, at the point where the river emptied into the bay, a high bluff rose from the water and the road ran about its foot.

Those who have tested it, know that there is no razor sharper than some of these thin cracked oyster-shells; and Conchita, in her half-shod condition, soon discovered this fact also.

Alderdyce made her lean on his arm, but it was of little assistance; he could feel how she winced and started again and again.

"I once read of a poor little mermaid who danced on knives," Conchita gasped at last; "I feel more sorry for her now."

Alderdyce stopped short. "This is impossible for you. Is there no way around?"

"No, this is the only road not far, far off; and see how dark it is growing, we must hasten on."

They struggled on again; but after a few steps, Conchita stumbled and fell forward with a cry of pain.

"Perhaps it is just as well it is dark," said Alderdyce, with decision; "for I should do the same in broad daylight."

The next moment he was walking on, carrying Conchita in his arms. Although she was too slight for her weight to be a burden to him, and his strength too steady to cause her uneasiness, neither spoke until he set her down at the bridge's edge; then she thanked him with an unaffected, simple gratitude which left Alderdyce bowing in spirit before the quick woman's instinct which taught even this unsophisticated child to distinguish between his first attempt to carry her and his last.

Mr. Santillana was standing at the gate of his garden, anxiously peering up and down the street through the darkness, when the figure for which he was watching came in sight. He walked quickly forward with an exclamation of relief, as Conchita's voice called to him, announcing her return.

"My little one, where have you been? Have you met with an accident?"

"The accident is all over now," she answered; "I am quite safe, Padre."

He caught her to him. "You are not hurt?"

"No, no," she cried, laughingly disengaging herself; "but I have brought some one home with me whom you must thank for that. This is my father, Mr. Alderdyce."

Mr. Santillana turned to the stranger courteously; his English had less accent than his daughter's, but it was not so ready.

"Pardon me; I am an anxious father and mother in one. Will you come into the house, and let me thank you there?"

The house stood in the centre of the garden, and was a square, stone structure with small, two-story wings set on either side, far enough away to make covered corridors necessary to join them to the main building.

The room into which Alderdyce was shown was a crescent-shaped hall with a number of doors opening into it; it was evidently used as a sitting-room, for it held a large, scholarly-looking writing-desk, and a work-table covered with all kinds of womanly belongings. Books and papers were scattered over tables and chairs in a confusion which just escaped untidiness. A hanging-lamp showed that the walls were covered with oil-paintings, simply framed, but selected with exquisite care.

"Look, Padre," cried Conchita, stepping into the circle of falling light, and holding back her dress; "look at my new shoes! Mr. Alderdyce made them for me. When I fell into the bog and lost mine, he pulled me out and brought me home."

"Then I have every reason to be grateful," said Mr. Santillana. "I was most anxious about my little one; she is growing into a wild fledgling, I fear. Where had you wandered, Conchita?"

Alderdyce could see that in her father's eyes she was still a mere baby, and also that when talking to him she unconsciously became more infantile.

"I was 't' other side Swanton,'" she answered, laughing; "now don't scold me, dearest."

Her father looked at her lovingly, passing his hand lightly over her hair. "On 't' other side Swanton,' alone, my child! If I could scold, it would be better for you, little one. But so far alone! That must not happen again, Conchita."

"You never told me not to go there."

"No; nor did I ever tell you not to cross Swanton in a tub, little sophist."

"Oh, nothing ever happens to me," the girl answered, lightly; "some one always comes. This time it was Mr. Alderdyce," she added, smiling at the artist as she spoke.

"Pardon me, but is it the artist, Anthony Alderdyce?" asked Mr. Santillana, eagerly turning.

"But yes, Padre; how did you know?"

"I know him very well indeed," he answered, holding out his hand cordially. "I can claim an old acquaintance in your first *salon* picture, Mr. Alderdyce; I longed for its possession."

The artist, who had little expected quite what he found in this retreat, took the extended hand with some embarrassment and a sense of guilt. The picture of Conchita in his case weighed on his conscience, and his colour rose when the girl herself spoke of it.

"I had almost forgotten,— Mr. Alderdyce has made a sketch of me."

"Of you? Where was it painted?"

"In the wood; and I have not seen it myself yet; but you shall see it first, Padre. I know you long to."

"I am certainly most anxious to see it," replied Mr. Santillana.

Though the words and manner carried no discourtesy, that they meant, "and I intend to," was evident to Alderdyce. He hesitated, a little nettled, and reluctant to place an unfinished work before eyes which, while set in a kindly face, he yet recognized as keen and critical.

"The painting is incomplete," he began.

"Then you can cover all except the figure," said Mr. Santillana, pleasantly; "you must acknowledge that my curiosity to see that is pardonable."

Alderdyce drew out the canvas.

"Ah!" exclaimed Mr. Santillana, as he looked at it,— "genuine foliage, genuine sunshine, genuine shadow."

He hung over the painting, enraptured; and with a not

unnatural triumph, Alderdyce saw that the artist-nature was roused to a point which swept away fatherly scruples. The enthusiast looked up with shining eyes.

"It takes a brush with a long handle to reach Truth in the bottom of her well," he said; "but you have it, — ah, but you have it, Mr. Alderdyce."

Conchita peeped over her father's shoulder, then whispered a word in his ear and stole from the room.

When she returned, Mr. Santillana was talking earnestly with the young artist; and as her entrance interrupted them, he turned to look at her in mock consternation.

Her dark gown was changed for a soft yellow-tinted muslin which gained colour from the bright yellow of the roses which were stuck in her bosom and in her dark hair.

"Why, this means dinner, does it not? and your message not yet delivered, Conchita. She is a severe head of the house, Mr. Alderdyce; and you will do me a kindness and save me a scolding, if you will accept this tardy invitation and dine with us."

Alderdyce looked down at his rough suit. "But I am no dinner guest," he said.

"If that be all, I can keep you in countenance; for I have been hunting my lost bit of silver in garret and cellar," returned Mr. Santillana, glancing in laughing reproach at his daughter. "I show plenty of whitewash and cobwebs in evidence, I am sure."

Conchita stood by, smiling at him over her yellow roses; and Alderdyce, trusting that he showed a sufficiently decent hesitation, accepted.

Throughout the dinner the two men continued their interrupted discussion. Conchita sat almost silent, but evidently happy in her father's enjoyment of this contact with a thoughtful mind in touch with the new methods and advanced work in the world from which he was now separated.

"Why is he buried alive in this slumbering community?" Alderdyce thought.

"My little one and I live like hermits here," Mr. Santillana said, sighing unconsciously as they rose from the table; "but perhaps we gain in one way more than we lose in another. Get your zither, Conchita, and let us have some music on the veranda."

Conchita obeyed, and with her zither in her lap, sat on the broad veranda steps in the moonlight.

"I have only read of a zither as yet," Alderdyce said, looking at the instrument with interest.

"Then you have still to hear the quaintest, most fairy-like music in the world," answered Mr. Santillana. "Play, Conchita."

Conchita softly touched the wires, and the tripping, tinkling sounds, crossing and interrupting one another harmoniously, dropped like flowing water from her fingers.

Alderdyce sat on the step below her, letting himself drift with the witchery of the sensuous lilt and swing of the strange music, and the glamour it threw over the player, who sat with bent head and rapt listening expression, like that of a praising angel, he thought. He roused himself when the sounds died away, hushed by the girl's hand laid with light silencing touch on the still vibrating strings, and urged her warmly to play again; but Conchita laid the zither aside, shaking her head.

"Yes, play for us once more, Conchita mia," said her

father; and again Alderdyce noticed that his manner was as if coaxing a refractory child.

"I have listened during a whole dinner," she said, reproachfully, "and I have played too, and now I want to talk; it makes my throat sore to be quiet so long."

"Then talk, by all means," said Mr. Santillana, laughing; "no one knew that you were suffering. What do you want to talk about? Suppose you tell me how you came to be 't' other side Swanton' to-day."

"I went there to fish; I thought I would catch something to surprise you for your dinner, Padre, and I lost my hook and line and caught nothing at all, — oh, yes, I did too," she added, suddenly, looking at Alderdyce with dancing eyes.

"Gently, gently, Conchita," cried Mr. Santillana. "It is very good of you not to be offended," he went on, seeing Alderdyce laughing. "Child, you belong in your nursery still."

"I am only flattered," said Alderdyce. "If I was caught as a dinner dish, and if, in turn, I caught a model, it was but a fair exchange."

"Shall you finish my picture, then?" Conchita asked, as he had hoped she would.

The artist looked at Mr. Santillana questioningly. "If your father will allow me," he answered, and then received, albeit a little late, a cordial permission.

"But, Padre, I have not yet told you all about my falling into the bog," Conchita continued, "and it was very interesting; you must listen, and, Mr. Alderdyce, you shall tell all that I do not remember."

Yet, in spite of these precautions against forgetfulness, when Alderdyce left the Santillana mansion late in the evening, there was something lingering in his memory which he did not remind her to mention; and his last waking thought was: "She told of everything like an innocent angel, except that oyster-shell road."

At the end of Mr. Santillana's garden was a vine-covered summer-house which served him as a summer studio; and there Alderdyce was soon a familiar figure. He had finished the picture of the glade; but Conchita had consented to sit for him again as model for a Pandora, and her father had willingly agreed.

"But your sketch is too elaborate, Alderdyce," he said, looking at the Pandora the artist was blocking out; "you will leave Ayre long before that is finished."

"No; when I came here, I was prepared to stay so long as material offered," Alderdyce answered. "I still have out-door work before me."

"Then may Ayre's woods and waters prove inexhaustible," said Mr. Santillana, satisfied; and Alderdyce laughingly thanked him, his conscience clear in spite of the fact that he had just telegraphed for extra luggage. By some tortuous reasoning to which, however honest the heart, the human brain seems never unequal, he contrived to reconcile his acts and words to his own satisfaction.

The Pandora progressed but slowly. Painting with lazy, happy touches, Alderdyce lingered over it consciously, — conscious also of a growing content, which he did not endanger by self-examination.

Thus the days came and went. Almost a month drifted away; and then suddenly, without any warning, the peace of the sittings in the old summer-house studio was gone.

Perhaps it was but a fleeting expression, perhaps a

lingering look or unconscious word; but the woman in Conchita awakened, calling out startled warnings as a watchman on the walls, and all the innocent, childish freedom of manner vanished, flying in behind fortifications which the new-born woman knew how to erect instinctively.

"This is simply imposing on you," said Alderdyce, at last, laying aside his brushes in the midst of a thoroughly unsatisfactory sitting. "You have not really been able to pose this week; you are letting me tire you out."

Conchita flushed and raised her head, resuming the pose which she had lost. "No, I am not at all tired," she said hastily.

The Pandora was represented standing with her empty open box in her hand, gazing up into space with wondering, wide-open eyes.

"I am not going to take the colour out of your face to put on my canvas," Alderdyce asserted.

"But I have told you that I was not tired; pray go on," she responded impatiently.

Alderdyce returned to his work, but in a little while laid down his brushes, smiling and shaking his head.

"Is it like you to hang your head? If you are not tired, you are out of tune in some way. We will put off work for to-day."

"I am not tired, and I am perfectly well. Was I wrong again?"

"I am afraid you were."

"Then it is because I am stupid and have lost the idea."

"No, no; wait until to-morrow and all will be right," answered Alderdyce, patiently.

"But waiting only frets me; do go on."

Alderdyce, looking troubled, obeyed silently.

"Let me show you what it is I want," he said presently, rising and walking toward her as he spoke. "This is it." He touched either side of her head lightly, raising it, and as he did so discovered that her eyes were still hidden from him by tears.

Conchita broke from him, but not before the tears had fallen on her cheeks, leaving her confused hazel eyes bared to his; and in that moment, with a searching, almost painfully swift consciousness, Alderdyce knew them as the eyes of the woman he loved, and knew that she loved him.

He was still standing in the first bewilderment of his discovery when Mr. Santillana entered the summer-house.

"What! crying, my little one! What is it, Alderdyce? Have we let her sit too long?"

"That and the hot day together, I think," answered Alderdyce, rousing.

Mr. Santillana took his child in his arms, soothing and caressing her.

"But it is nothing; I do not know what it is myself," Conchita cried, half laughing, as her father wiped away her tears. "I must cry sometimes; and if I have nothing to cry for, I must cry for nothing."

Mr. Santillana looked at her anxiously. "We all have our moods at times," he said. "No more painting to-day, though. What do you say to eating our supper in the wood this evening? You might take us to your glade 't' other side Swanton,' Alderdyce."

Conchita slipped from her father's arm, and turned away. "I don't know," she objected; "picnics are so much spiders and worms."

Mr. Santillana again looked at her anxiously. "You

are over-tired," he said reassuringly. "If you don't like spiders and worms, you must learn to; it 's a healthy taste. Yes, we shall go this afternoon."

But that afternoon the rain clouds blew in from the north, south, east, and west, and by alternately breaking, banking, and opening, kept the land wet for a week.

The picnic was postponed daily, but Conchita would not permit the painting to be laid aside; she insisted that she was quite well, that the work would never be finished at that rate, and repeatedly asked Alderdyce to set a date for its completion.

The young artist, who was unusually silent, would promise nothing definite; and Conchita clung too tenaciously to her father's side to make any explanation possible, even had he deemed it advisable.

For some days the progress on the Pandora was confined to the drapery, as Conchita sat always with lowered eyes and drooping head, and Alderdyce would ask for no change; but at last, by deliberately outmanœuvring, he gained a half-hour alone with his model, and took advantage of it to absorb himself in his colours, speaking to her only as a secondary consideration. Through this consistent behaviour, and a guarded care in words and looks he finally had the reward of seeing the painful consciousness under his gaze fade away, and the old confidence return.

"The first dry day shall be for the picnic," said Mr. Santillana each morning; and "Until the picnic," thought Alderdyce each day, "and not until then, however great the temptation."

At last the clouds scattered, the sun shone with redoubled power, and there came a day seemingly created for the woods.

"So this is the historic glade, Alderdyce," said Mr. Santillana, looking about him.

The picnic "t' other side Swanton" was in full swing. A gypsy kettle hung bubbling and boiling over a glowing fire; the supper, spread out on fresh-gathered leaves and little squares of white paper, stood invitingly near, ready to be eaten when the tea had drawn.

"We shall have no clearing away of plates," Conchita had decided; "we shall eat from nothing which cannot be burned up afterwards."

She set the grassy table herself and helped Alderdyce gather brands for the burning, dragging in great armfuls of brushwood to her father, who had constituted himself stoker. The veriest child could have been no more delighted with the potatoes which Alderdyce roasted in the ashes and the eggs which he wrapped in wet paper and baked under the hot logs.

"She is as excited as if at a ball," he thought, watching her delightedly.

But the preparations were so elaborate, and the supper eaten so lingeringly, that Mr. Santillana began looking restlessly at his watch before the meal was over.

"Do you think we shall reach town before the evening mail goes out, Alderdyce?" he asked.

Alderdyce looked at the hour reluctantly. "Not unless we leave this moment," he answered, but not offering to move. "Have you letters to send?"

"Yes; some which must go by to-night."

"No, no, Padre," cried Conchita; "let them lie until to-morrow. Look at the long, queer shadows, and the firelight just beginning to show against them, — this is the best hour."

"Then stay and enjoy it," said Mr. Santillana, rising. "But don't let it be long, Alderdyce. I must go, and by short cuts. Conchita, you may stay a little longer, if Mr. Alderdyce will bring you home."

"With pleasure," the artist answered quietly.

He watched Conchita closely, expecting her hasty retreat; but she only sat contentedly by the fire, poking its red embers with a stick while stating that it needed another armful of bark.

Alderdyce accompanied Mr. Santillana to the edge of the glade, and returned with a load of bark which made the flames shoot high in the air.

"Come with me," he said; "I have found something to show you."

"Something to show me, — what is it?"

"Come and see," he answered mysteriously.

He led the way to the spot where the wooden sandals had been carved out a month before.

"Do those look familiar?" he asked, pointing to the ground.

Conchita looked down to see what had once been her shoes, lying where she had flung them the day they encountered the bog to their sore defeat. The grass had grown in about them, and the rain had beaten them into the earth; but Alderdyce picked them up as carefully as though they still had value.

"These are the mutual acquaintances who introduced us," he said; "if they were only a trifle smaller I would wear them on my watch-chain as a charm; as it is, they shall at least have Christian burial."

With laughing respect he carried the shoes to the bog, and thrust them deep down in the soft earth, saying to Conchita as he did so. —

"Bid them farewell; they have seen the first chapter, but no one save ourselves shall see the second."

She smiled and flushed, but answered nothing. The firelight was flickering and leaping up in little tongues of flame as they walked back toward it.

"We must scatter it carefully before we go,—it might do damage," Alderdyce said; "but not quite yet."

They stood looking into the red embers, speaking on any subject except the one which was the central thought in the heart of each.

As Conchita bent over the fire, the jewelled dagger which she always wore, and which Alderdyce had grown to regard as almost a part of her, dropped at her feet. He picked it up, and replacing it in her hair, half expected her quick withdrawal; but again, though her colour rose, she said nothing; she was making no effort now to ignore or repulse. In the mutual understanding which seemed suddenly established between them, all trace of startled womanhood or childish petulance vanished. Alderdyce dreaded breaking the charm.

At last Conchita spoke softly, as if afraid of jarring the stillness which had fallen upon them. "We must go home now, must we not? The Padre will be anxious again."

Alderdyce assented, opening the blazing logs, thrusting them apart, and scattering the embers.

"The woods and the lights and the shadows are all just as they were the day we first walked home together," he said, looking back as they left the place; "we might almost think it was that first day, except for ourselves."

They followed the winding path down the wooded hill, with only a short, unspoken word separating them,—a word too near the lips, too often half uttered, not to be a conscious presence.

The oyster-shell road stretched out at the foot of the bluff, a curving white line in the dusk as they looked down on it from above.

"There is the shell road now," Alderdyce said; "we are nearly home."

The slight, crushing sound of the shells beneath their feet startled a blackbird, which flew up from the road before them with a shrill cry and flapping of wings.

Conchita started back, and then laughed tremulously. "It was so sudden," she explained, as Alderdyce paused also and stood by her, holding her hand in his.

"It was only a blackbird; but see, here are the same sharp oyster-shells; do you remember how I carried you over them in my arms?"

"Yes," she whispered breathlessly.

She turned from him, and would have walked on, but he gently prevented her. He could count the pulsations of her heart in her quick breaths.

"Surely you can trust me now," he said. "Dear, I have something to tell you; will you listen?"

Close by the blackbird dropped down in the road again, where its mate joined it. The soft winnowing of their wings was in the air, and the presence of new vows and new words set to the old faltering, whispering melody which is always in tune.

"What has happened?" thought Alderdyce, rousing the next morning with a start. He had known, even in his fortunate life, what it meant to wake suddenly from sleep with the recollection of a heavy heart. "Joy and grief have some kindred touch, then," he decided, smiling as he remembered the events of the evening before.

Conchita had insisted on his leaving her at the door of her home, as she claimed the right to speak to her father first. "Your eyes talk," she said; "they would tell all before I could."

A little pity for the lonely man whose ewe lamb he was stealing mingled with Alderdyce's thoughts, as he walked out to the Santillana mansion to assert his claim. He wondered how Conchita had fared in telling her news, — if her father had helped her shyness, and what each had said.

"He had no surprise, at least," he thought with satisfaction; "all has gone on in his sight, — almost all, that is."

There was no one sitting in the crescent-shaped hall when Alderdyce entered it, though usually the father and daughter were both there at that hour. He shortly received a message from Mr. Santillana, however, asking his presence in his private study.

"To be treated to a little Spanish formality and grandeeism," the young man decided with some amusement.

Mr. Santillana's study was in the left wing of the building, and his daughter's apartments occupied the right. Alderdyce remembered how on first taking him over the queer old house, Mr. Santillana had showed him the rooms in the right wing, pointing out one as "my child's nursery." "Will he persist in calling her a baby to-day?" the artist wondered; and he was still smiling at the thought when he entered the study.

Mr. Santillana was seated behind his table, and did not come forward to greet his guest, although he rose with his usual careful courtesy.

"I can scarcely decide which of us has been to blame, Mr. Alderdyce, — you for changing my child into a woman, or I for not recognizing the fact," he began, as though continuing an unfinished conversation, and speaking in a strained, unnatural manner.

Alderdyce, looking at him in surprise, saw that his face seemed old and as gray as his hair, while each line in it was accentuated.

"Why should either be blamed?" he asked, with a sudden chill and depression.

"You will do me the justice to believe that I was wholly surprised by what I learned last night," Mr. Santillana went on.

"But there was no intent to deceive you," Alderdyce interrupted hastily. "You have surely known what kept me here."

"No; on that point I was wholly deceived."

The colour rose hotly in the young artist's face. "I repeat that there was no intent to deceive you; and if Conchita spoke to you when she returned last night, as I suppose she did, you knew all within an hour after it was settled."

"My daughter did tell me last night of the matter under discussion."

Alderdyce coloured again. "I should, perhaps, have spoken to you first under all the circumstances," he said frankly; "but I interpreted your consent to our daily intercourse as approval."

Mr. Santillana winced, and his face grew a shade whiter. "I have been culpably careless; my only excuse is my blindness, which is an excuse no longer. My precautions come late; but I must ask you when it is your intention to leave Ayre, as until then my daughter is of necessity house-bound?"

In spite of what had already passed, Alderdyce stood incredulous of his own hearing. "Is it possible that I comprehend you? Am I to understand that you refuse your consent, now?" he asked.

"I absolutely refuse it."

"On what ground?"

"It is my unalterable decision."

The artist looked for a moment of silent amazement into the inflexible face before him.

"You will let me ask a few questions, Mr. Santillana?" he said quietly; adding, as he received no immediate answer, "I think I may claim in justice so much as that."

Mr. Santillana sat down behind his table again, with a gesture of assent. There was a weariness in his attitude, Alderdyce thought, as he took his seat by the opposite side.

Mr. Santillana spoke first. "It is but fair to warn you that nothing to be said or left unsaid can make a change."

"Have you come to any knowledge of me or my life which obliges this decision?"

"None."

"I think I may safely say that I could disprove any calumnies."

"Of that I am equally sure."

"Then am I not reasonable in considering that I have the right to know your grounds of objection?"

"Most reasonable; and most unreasonably I refuse to give them, now and forever. This is my final decision, Mr. Alderdyce."

But as Mr. Santillana spoke, he might have seen a gradual change on the face of the younger man, and have recognized an expression different from his own because of a difference of feature and temperament, but still the reflection of a resolution as deliberate and unconceding.

The massive, still face at one side of the table, and the thin, nervously determined one opposite, looked each into each steadily. Although there was a strange lack of antagonism in words and manner, both knew in that moment that this was the beginning of a struggle between them, as desperate and perhaps as hopeless as the battling of the stags on the mountain-side with their antlers interlocked.

"What has the woman who last night promised to be my wife said?"

Mr. Santillana's hand shaded his eyes suddenly; but there was no faltering in his voice as he answered, "She is my child, and she will obey me."

"She is no child to-day; she is a woman, and has proven it. She must decide between us."

But here the contest ceased to be equal; on this point, the father was in a position of vantage from which he was not to be shaken.

"She will not see you again," he said, rising; "it will be wiser for her to have less to remember. And, Mr. Alderdyce, this is a worse than useless discussion."

"It is equally useless to think of its ending here," Alderdyce answered; "and I can only regard it as ended for the hour."

As he left the house, Alderdyce fell back again into his first bewilderment; Mr. Santillana's attitude appeared to him even more incomprehensible than at first. He spent the rest of the day wandering about in the woods of Ayre, pondering the situation, though unable to arrive at any conclusion except the hopelessness of solving a difficulty and a mystery where no clew could be gained. Nevertheless, the thought of leaving Ayre and Conchita did not occur to him.

When he returned to his lodgings, late in the evening, he had once more sought an interview with Mr. Santillana, and been denied admission at the door,—a possibility which he had not considered.

The first thing which caught his eye on entering his own room, was the painting of Conchita in the glade; he had set it out on his easel before leaving in the morning. Now, plunged in thought, but not yet discouraged, he sat down before it again, and if with not quite the surety of the morning, still with the ability to dream out the building of his future life with Conchita as the corner-stone.

He saw her in his home and among his friends; he pictured her delight in the world he would show her,—guardedly, not as he knew it, though seeing it through his eyes.

He lived over and over again the evening before, and smiled, remembering Conchita's struggles when he tried to teach her soft Spanish tongue the harsh letters of his name. "Alderdyce" had always been an effort to her; "Anthony" now seemed impossible. She made the words sound like her native language by her pronunciation, and paused before each one as if to arrange lip and tongue before speaking.

"Anthony!"

Alderdyce almost started from his chair; for a moment he thought he heard Conchita's voice speaking near him.

"This is the lover, I suppose," he decided with amusement; and as he reached this conclusion, again, only this time more distinctly, he heard the voice which he could not mistake, with the accent he knew so well, calling his name. He sprang from his chair to the door, and opened it.

Conchita, her face white and her eyes wide with unspeakable wretchedness, stood on his threshold.

"My child will obey me," Mr. Santillana had said, and believed; but there had not been peace in his household.

Conchita, thwarted for the first time in her untrammelled life, found her tears and entreaties of no avail. Her father's gentle, unyielding resolution maddened her by its very gentleness. The passionate Southern blood, until now slumbering in her veins, roused to wild reproaches and accusations of cruelty.

Mr. Santillana stood aghast at the storm which he was only able to control by stern words, — the first his child had ever heard from his lips.

Conchita sobbed herself to sleep that night, wounded and resentful; and none of her dreams told her of the figure which stole in, after night was morning, to kneel in the darkness by her bedside, nor of the slow, hot tears that dropped on her head, each representing a deeper sorrow than all that she had ever shed.

The next day the same scenes were enacted over and over.

By some instinct, Conchita knew of her lover's presence in the house on both occasions; and her entreaties to see him, if for once only, were piteous. Her father's drawn features bore witness of his sufferings, though his determination remained unshaken.

That Conchita's vehemence gradually subsided into broken pleadings and quivering lips made her the stronger; but she seemed calmer, more controlled, when she parted from her father at night, and with that slight comfort, worn in body and mind, Mr. Santillana went to his bed and slept the heavy sleep of exhaustion.

When he woke on the morrow, it was only with a weary shrinking from the struggle of another day. He sat waiting in the breakfast-room, longing for yet dreading Conchita's coming, which was delayed later than usual.

Her father had just decided to send for her, when he heard her light, flying step in the hall, so different from the listless footfall of yesterday that he looked up eagerly, and as the door opened saw a sight which he never forgot.

The dark oak doorway was framing Conchita's figure; her long red cape, her red cap, her face all alight and flushed, her brilliant eyes and parted lips, — she stood for an irresolute instant poised like a vibrating flame on the threshold. Then she flashed suddenly across the room, to fling her arms about her father's neck, and hide her face on his shoulder.

Mr. Santillana rose, thrusting her from him, yet grasping her wrist in his hand. Over his child's shoulder he had seen Alderdyce enter also.

"What does this mean?" he asked. He glanced at Conchita's cap and wrapping. "Where have you been?" he demanded harshly. "Child, what have you dared to do?"

The girl cowered before the white heat of his indignation, and shrank with a cry of pain at his grasp.

With a quick motion Alderdyce threw his arm about

her, drawing her toward him. "She is my wife, Mr. Santillana," he said; "we were married last night."

Mr. Santillana dropped Conchita's hand, and stood staring dumbly at the two figures before him, the wife clinging fearfully to her husband, who was standing protectingly between him and his child. He turned from them with a gesture of despair to sink into his chair, covering his stricken face with his hands.

Conchita broke from Alderdyce's arms, and threw herself on her knees before her father. Her arms were again clasped about his neck, not to be loosened; her lips were at his ear, passionately imploring forgiveness. She drew his hands away, and laid her tear-stained cheek against his own.

Alderdyce only waited to see the father bend and fold her in his arms; then he went from the room silently, leaving them together. When he returned, Conchita was still nestling close to her father's breast, sitting on his knee with her head resting against his shoulder.

Putting her gently aside, Mr. Santillana rose and held out his hand. "Conchita has confessed all," he said.

"And am I also to be forgiven?"

"You must know that I have nothing to forgive; what is, is. Will you try to wipe the memory of yesterday from the slate, Alderdyce?"

The younger man's face spoke his relief, as their hands met in a cordial grasp.

"And now," Mr. Santillana continued, with a lightness that but slightly veiled his emotion, "we must eat the wedding-breakfast; it has been cooling on the table for an hour, and will taste more like funeral baked meats, I fear. Come, Conchita; come, my children."

It was a strange wedding-breakfast, and a stranger honeymoon which followed.

The day after the marriage Mr. Santillana had a piece of news to break to them on his side. He announced that he meant to return to Spain for a brief visit. His property at home had long been calling for his personal supervision, he said; and what better time than now, when Conchita's marriage seemed to pave the way to the performance of this long-neglected duty.

Conchita was in despair at the thought of such a separation. In marrying Alderdyce, parting from her father had never entered her mind; but Mr. Santillana stood firm in his decision, and with this journey in view, Conchita would not consent to leave him even for the conventional wedding-trip, and Alderdyce did not urge it. The cloud which had arisen between Mr. Santillana and himself was dispelled as if it had never been.

Genuinely American, Alderdyce only remembered the strange contest in the study, to put it down to some "queer foreign notion," and then dismiss it wholly from his mind.

They walked through the woods, they rode and drove over each mile of surrounding country, and spent whole days boating on Swanton.

"Essence of lotus leaves, — essence of lotus leaves; it is in the air one breathes walking through the dear old grass-grown streets," said Alderdyce.

Conchita looked up from her zither, which lay in her lap. She sat in the bottom of the boat, which was drifting down Swanton to Ayre; her father was holding the rudder-ropes, and Alderdyce was idly leaning on his oars.

"Our honeymoon has been different and nicer than any ever before," she said.

"Utterly different and infinitely nicer," echoed her husband, as she waited for his assent.

"We have been chaperoned, for one thing," she went on, smiling back at her father, "and we have made our wedding-journey in little bits every day. We shall have travelled as many miles as most people when we finish, shall we not, Anthony?"

"Anthony," repeated Mr. Santillana, mimicking her accent; "I can pronounce your husband's name better than his wife can, little one."

"Ask her to tell you her own name," laughed Alderdyce.

"I can say it much better now," Conchita answered with dignity. "Mrs. Anthony Alderdyce," she repeated slowly, hopelessly broadening the vowels and softening the consonants. "What does it matter?" she cried, striking the chords of her zither to drown the two men's laughter. "Listen!"

She began a half-gay, half-plaintive, little Spanish love-song, in which the water lapping on the boat's side, the splash of a rising fish, and the bird's cries on the river-bank, seemed but a part.

"Los suspiros son aire y van al aire,
Las lágrimas son agua y van al mar;
Dime, mujer; cuando el amor se olvida,
¿Sabes tú adonde vá?"

"Sighs are but breath, and are lost in the air;
Tears are but water, and lost in the tides.
Tell me, O woman, when love is forgotten,
Dost know where it hides?"

"Let others say my name as they may," said Conchita, as the song ended; "I am the only one who can *be* it, am I not, Anthony?"

Alderdyce bent and kissed her, laughing again. "You blessed baby!" he said, "does that still rankle? Play me a measure now to row by."

So they walked through their Arcadia hand in hand, with an Arcadian simplicity of which the man was as blissfully conscious as the woman was blissfully unconscious.

The Pandora was a finished work, and a wonderfully living likeness; Mr. Santillana's preparations for his journey were ended; and still Alderdyce's studio and the work which was awaiting his home-coming lay neglected.

The effort to break this charmed existence was wanting on his part, and the resolution to hasten the separation was lacking with Mr. Santillana; but at last the final day of the rapidly waning honeymoon was selected as the date for sundering old ties and entering into a new life for all.

It was agreed among them that the dreaded separation should be a topic sent to Coventry; and though their gayety was at times a mere drapery about sadness, perhaps those last summer days, with the end so near, were the happiest of all, — fuller of loving memories and a closer clinging of hearts.

"To-morrow we part, children," said Mr. Santillana. "Conchita, you must leave us alone to-night. You will need all the sleep you can snatch for your journey, little one; go to your room and rest. Do you come with me to my study, Alderdyce."

The father and his child's husband sat in the quiet study, talking over their separate plans for the future.

"Come and live with us," Alderdyce had urged over and over.

But Mr. Santillana had always contrived to put the question by. Now he made no secret of his decision to spend the greater part of what remained of his life in his own land

"Conchita need not be told this," he said; "I can visit you at times, but my home must be Spain."

"Do you really dare trust Conchita alone with me?" asked Alderdyce, smiling. "Although I still hope to change your mind, I must thank you for the confidence you show."

"I have great confidence in you," answered Mr. Santillana, gravely; "and yet —" An expression of troubled thought passed over his features; he sat silent for a time, and then rose and left the room, returning in a few moments with a bottle of wine and two glasses in his hand.

"Will you drink a toast with me?" he asked.

"If the inside is what the outside promises, I certainly will, be the toast what it may," Alderdyce answered.

"This wine has been used at every wedding in our family since its vintage, in 1807. The wedding-toast has always been drunk in it, and now yours shall be."

But Mr. Santillana's grave face was not wearing the expression for a wedding loving-cup, Alderdyce thought, as he watched him uncorking the bottle and filling the glasses. The rich golden sherry was forming in little oily beads against the smooth side, as Mr. Santillana took the stem of his glass in his fingers and without lifting it spoke slowly, —

"Once I asked you to wipe out all memory of a conversation which took place in this room; now I ask you to recall, if possible, every word that passed."

Alderdyce rose instantly, in quiet but extreme surprise, and stood waiting for what should follow so strange a preface. Mr. Santillana went on, —

"It may help you to understand better the toast I wish to propose."

He paused a moment, and then lifting his wine-glass, looked over it, speaking in a repressed, excited voice, yet still with great deliberation: —

"By every effort, I opposed my child's marriage to you; now, whatever the outcome, may you be forever blessed or forever cursed as you treat her well or ill."

The sharp click of Alderdyce's glass against his own, his indignant eyes, his quick "amen," all came as a hot retort; yet when the two glasses were set down, Mr. Santillana's face had cleared. He turned and laid his hand on Alderdyce's arm with an almost caressing gesture, saying, —

"When you have daughters of your own, you may understand."

"Must I wait until then?" asked Alderdyce, coldly.

"You cannot forgive a father's doubts and fears then, Anthony?"

The winning sweetness of voice and manner were too much his daughter's for Alderdyce to resist.

"You may trust me wholly," he answered, melting; "I wish you could have done so unquestioningly, that is all."

"Perhaps I fear most from Conchita," Mr. Santillana said thoughtfully; "she has shown herself as passionately determined as she is gentle. You will be very tender of her, Anthony; but you must be as tender as a lover, and as watchful as a father *should* be, not as I have been. And now, having asked you to be more than mortal, I have done."

They separated for the night, each grave with the gravity of what had passed, but with the consciousness that the confidence between them had not been weakened; and their farewells the next day were none the less regretfully sincere.

Conchita broke down utterly at the last moment. She looked around the familiar, crescent-shaped hall with longing, half-frightened eyes, and then clung about her father's neck, refusing to go to the carriage which waited at the door.

"I have only known Anthony for two months, and I have loved you for seventeen years," she sobbed.

Mr. Santillana clasped her to him with an agony beyond tears; he kissed over and over again the lips which pleaded to stay, and then gently loosening her clinging hands, he laid them in her husband's and hurried from the room. The parting was over. The new life began with the crossing of the old home's threshold, and the old life ended with the closing of the door.

Almost two years had passed since Conchita's marriage, and though in all that time Mr. Santillana had been in America but once, and then for a short time only, Conchita found it impossible to be as distressed as she felt she ought to be at the change.

"It is not Ayre, and my father is not here, and yet—Anthony, I cannot understand it; I am ashamed to be so happy," she would say.

It would have required an effort on the part of most women to be unhappy in her surroundings. The whirling life of a great city had at first bewildered her eyes and mind, accustomed to the sleepy stillness of Ayre; but she soon learned to peep out into the new world with a timid curiosity, until what had seemed strange and unnatural became as second nature. She spent the greater part of her days in her husband's studio, which had been only an old brick stable set in a court behind their home; but Alderdyce had evolved from it a studio of studios. The building remained unchanged outside, except that the door was new, and bore a huge old-fashioned brass-knocker.

Inside the whole was altered. The loft was torn out, with the exception of a strip across the doorway which was reached by ladder-steps, and served as a shelf for Conchita's piano and growing plants. Draperies, hanging from its outer edge to the floor, cut off a portion of the room; the old windows were boarded over, and one as large as safety admitted, was cut in the north wall. There was no useless endeavour to make the interior appear finished; the rough rafters of the roof were visible, and the rude bricks and mortar were only concealed by a coat of venetian-red paint. The fittings of the studio were, however, individual and unique, and its chief charm to the knowing lay in its atmosphere of genuine work, not to be created by any affectation of workmanlike surroundings, however artistically arranged. In a place of honour, on one of the walls, hung the beautiful Pandora, repeated by a mirror hanging opposite. An open fire and a commodious divan formed what was known as Conchita's corner,—for there she and her zither were at home.

Alderdyce had cared too little for general society to

introduce his wife there; but among the inner Israel of artists and professional men who frequented his studio, Conchita was a well-known figure. In this critical little kingdom, where some wore purple and fine linen, and others threadbare coats, her success had been marked enough to have startled her had she realized it; but though few have chariot-wheels that unwittingly take captives, she never lost the innocent unconsciousness which constituted her chief charm.

Almost two years of married life had passed before the autocratic baby first showed his face in the household, and Conchita rejoiced doubly in his coming, as she hoped to lure her father to her side by the news of a grandson's arrival; but even these wonderful tidings only brought a letter in reply, over which the young mother shed tears of disappointment. She had set her heart on laying her baby in her father's arms. "Write to him again, Anthony; tell him he must come, — there is nothing else on earth that I need to wish for now," she said.

"Then, if you have but one earthly wish, I may write to Spain that you are tolerably happy, may I not?" asked Alderdyce.

"Write that I am happier than happy, my husband."

"And also that I treat you fairly well? Your father will wish particularly to know that."

Conchita laughed the idle, ready laugh of a light heart. "I shall write myself that you abuse me. Do you think that would bring him home, Anthony?"

"No, not when the news of this miraculous bundle did not," Alderdyce answered, bending to take the soft, limp, little body from the mother's arms.

"Where have you hidden him?" he asked, searching

among the wrappings for the tiny face of his first-born. "And to think that this is alive, and my son, my prototype! I suppose man needs to be shown occasionally from what he comes. Come here, Impertinence!"

Conchita looked on nervously.

"But ah, be careful, dearest; you will break him!"

"Well, is n't he mine? I am going to take him for his first walk, and show him the world he is to fit in his sling."

"You must take him up the stairs first, then, Anthony; and — Oh, wait, dear, there is more to arrange; I have the little Bible and bit of money all ready somewhere."

"A wife and a mother, and no years of discretion yet, Conchita. What mumbo-jumbo is this, you superstitious child?"

"The money in one hand, and the Bible in the other, and up in the world first; it should always be so, Anthony. Stop laughing and hold him close to me."

Alderdyce watched her delighted face as the baby-fingers closed convulsively over the coin. "See how wise he is! he understands," she cried; "and now —"

"Let us hope he does not," laughed the father, as the Bible fell to the floor. "There, don't be troubled, dear heart; see, he is clutching both like a practical Christian. Now for the triumphal procession."

"Are these your heathen rites, then, my children?" said a voice behind them; and Conchita, turning with a cry of joy, was clasped in her father's arms.

"My heart kept pulling and pulling you here, and so you have come, Padre."

"And so I have come; you know how it is yourself now, little one. Show me the child, my beloved."

Mr. Santillana had arrived by the same steamer which brought his letter. At the last moment, it seemed, he had found it impossible to stay away, and he had hurriedly taken passage for America and arrived without notice in the happy triangular household, to be cooed over by Conchita, and warmly welcomed by Alderdyce.

For the first few days after his coming there was little thought of beyond the joys of reunion; but Alderdyce soon decided that the father looked older and careworn.

"You are missing Conchita, Mr. Santillana," he said; "why not stay with us altogether? You have made the break now, let it rest so."

"Now that I have him, he shall not slip from me again," Conchita declared, holding fast by his hand. "You will stay, Padre, will you not? Ah, why do you wish to go?"

Mr. Santillana smiled sadly.

"You have yet to learn what duty's *must* means, my child; I shall stay as long as I may, be sure. But you have not yet seen what I have for my grandson," he added quickly, seeing Conchita's eyes fill with tears; "here it is, open it for him."

Conchita opened the odd-shaped package which he gave her, with curiosity. Its outward semblance was only a common little earthenware pot; but as she raised the lid, the contents proved to be a quantity of gold pieces.

"He shall start life with a pot of money, however he may end," Mr. Santillana said, smiling at the fact that Conchita's delight in the conceit was far greater than her pleasure in its more tangible value.

"You shall keep the gold, Anthony," she said, carelessly pouring it out into his hands; "all but this largest piece, that he shall cut his teeth on, and the gold-pot shall be his powder-box, if only the puff fits. Do you try it, Padre."

Mr. Santillana, amused by the little womanly arrangements, turned over the contents of the baby's basket, searching for the puff; suddenly he started and looked up.

"Where did you get this?" he asked. He was holding up a copy of Ibsen's plays. "Have you read this, Conchita?"

"No; I found them on the table, and put them by to read."

Mr. Santillana walked quickly toward the fireplace with the book in his hand, and a moment later the volume would have been in the flames, had not Alderdyce called out a protest.

"They won't hurt my morals, Mr. Santillana. I was reading the plays myself; I promise to take them out to the studio where Conchita won't see them."

Mr. Santillana drew back and laid the volume down. "Perhaps I am forgetting that it is your wife and your book and your house," he said, his colour rising slightly.

"'Todo ello es de Usted,' including the baby," answered Alderdyce, good-humouredly; "and I hope that sounds familiar and makes you feel at home at the same time. You may burn every book in the house if you will only stay."

But in spite of urging from Alderdyce, and almost forcible detention from Conchita, Mr. Santillana persisted in his intention of speedy return. He had seen Conchita surrounded by devoted friends, the centre of her husband's heart, her life filled and rounded by the new cares of motherhood; and he left the more easily because he could not doubt the sure foundations on which her happiness rested.

And yet, the very night after his departure, those foundations were shaken to the centre. The little life which seemed too small to be the cope-stone, was suddenly withdrawn. There was no time for preparation, hardly any warning. It was all over with merciful quickness, the physician said; but Alderdyce, stunned and heart-sick, looking at the stricken mother, could see no mercy anywhere.

He had found it hardly possible to make Conchita realize the truth; only after he took the lifeless little body from her arms did her bewildered mind seem to grasp her loss. The terror of the shock appeared literally to hold her in its clutch; she cowered under it as from a physical blow.

Alderdyce had no time for his own grief in ministering to hers. He thought for her, lived for her, tended her every moment in those days of despair.

"Take her away, Mr. Alderdyce," the physician counselled; "mentally and bodily she must have instant change." And Alderdyce, ready to seek any remedy, hurried his wife to the seaside. The spring was advancing and he hoped everything from the long hours when he kept her out of doors basking in the sun on the rocks.

Before long the faint colour which rose in her cheeks gave him new courage. She grew calmer also, and would sit by his side silent for hours, looking out over the sea with sad eyes, yet gaining comfort from it, Alderdyce thought, until one gray morning when he knew differently. They were sitting on the rocks together, Conchita silent as ever and Alderdyce watching the scene before them with an artist's delight; the sun had been shining fitfully and feebly, but now the sharp sea-air was striking in their faces, the gray stretch of water merged into the gray of the horizon, and the sky was full of low-hanging clouds scudding before the rising wind. A thin line of angry, dull yellow lay in the east, whence the wind came.

In the distance, battling and fluttering, a small white-winged vessel was struggling for harbour, while the boom of the swelling breakers beat with a troubled pulse, like rhythm, on the shore.

"That boat is in some danger," said Alderdyce, at last, rising to his feet; "it would do better headed for the open sea."

Almost as he spoke, he was startled by Conchita's voice in an outbreak of wild sorrow and lamenting.

"Oh, take me away!" was the burden. She sat with her hands over her ears, shutting out the voice of the sea; in its murmurs she heard her baby's crying, and its deeper tones frightened her.

Alderdyce vainly tried to soothe her. "But you are better, dearest; see how much stronger than when you came."

"I am afraid,—afraid," she whispered. "Ah, Anthony, take me home!"

"Afraid of what, dear love?"

"That awful sea, it is taking my baby from me; but I shall surely remember him when I am home again. Oh, take me there, Anthony; take me home!"

Alderdyce, with a sudden pallor on his face, lifted her head from his breast, and looked deep into her eyes; as he did so, the shadow of the fear which was in them grew into his.

"You shall go home now, if you will," he replied, gently soothing her.

As they moved away, he glanced back once more.

Far off in the distance, a tiny white speck showed that the little vessel was yielding to the untempered wind, and seeking refuge in the open sea. The scene stamped itself indelibly on his brain, and he carried it away with him then and forever after.

Mr. Santillana had found the cable telling of his grandson's death awaiting him on reaching Spain, and had cabled in reply that he would return by the next steamer. Alderdyce built much on the prospect of his presence. In her own home, Conchita had certainly grown stronger; but as the excitement of the grief passed, a settled melancholy and childish petulance seemed to take its place.

She would consent to no medical attention; and her physician, judging it wiser to humour her, received his report through her husband, who yielded to every whim with a tender patience which he felt was hopelessly inadequate, for the end was always a scene of passionate self-reproach on Conchita's part, and then the weary round over again. She had ceased speaking of her baby; and after once breaking what he felt to be a dangerous silence, Alderdyce dared not repeat the agitating experiment.

From the constant strain on nerves, mind, and heart, and the brooding fear of he knew not what, he was looking more of an invalid than Conchita when at last the ship on which Mr. Santillana had sailed was sighted as due that same evening.

Alderdyce carried the news to Conchita, watching her

awakened interest hopefully, as she asked over and over of the exact hour when her father might be expected to arrive.

She prepared his room herself, and would let no one else enter it. With a heart full of thankfulness, Alderdyce saw her looking and acting once more like herself. The ugly wordless fears which had raised their heads and haunted him, were laid to rest.

She had almost turned from him in her self-absorption, but now this was changed also; she seemed to crave his presence, his touch; and when, toward evening, he was forced to leave her to meet a pressing engagement, she clung to him with tender words and kisses which stirred him strangely. Even then he would have lingered had she not sent him from her.

"You must go, dear love; for I must sleep before my father comes," she said, smiling. "I have been a great care to you, dearest; but from now I shall care for myself. Kiss me once more and go."

Alderdyce left her reluctantly, and detained by his engagement longer than he had expected, hurried home, facing a gorgeous sunset. He walked with a lighter step and a lighter heart than he had known for weeks. The clouds in the west glowed, as he looked at them, with more and more beauty.

"Conchita must see this," he thought, "even if I wake her for it."

He ran up the stairs to her room, three steps at once, calling her, but the rooms were empty; and seeing the key of the studio taken from its place, he knew that he should find her there, as in the habit of happier days. He walked quickly across the courtyard, and opened the lock with his latch-key.

"Where are you?" he called, as he entered, and was met by silence and a closed door; the inner door, which always stood open, was shut, and as he turned the handle in the lock, it resisted.

"Conchita!"

There was a sudden stillness, as if all creation held its breath with him, listening; and then Alderdyce heard a strange voice, which he yet knew as his own, whisper, "Not that, my God, not that!"

In those moments, standing with his hand on the lock, he knew all that he had feared, all that he had fought, fearing. The future, the other side of those wooden panels, held no shock, only fulfilment.

He reeled for a moment, and then the weakness passed. He stepped back and flung the full force of his body on the door until it groaned beneath the blows of his foot and shoulder; the lock broke suddenly, and he was in the room.

Her cheek pillowed softly on her hand, her eyes closed, her lips apart as if she breathed gently in her sleep, Conchita lay on the divan by the fireplace.

Thus Alderdyce had seen her sleep a thousand times; and yet he knew, before he caught her to him, that her head would lie lifeless in his bosom, and her lips breathless beneath his,—knew that there would be coldness in the very warmth of her body, that her heart would be silent under his searching hand.

He moved as one in a waking dream, knowing that each anticipating thought must be fulfilled. The vial which stood by the couch was no surprise; with every sense sharpened, its opium odour was in his nostrils before he drew the stopper, and he felt it must be there ever after.

He knelt, holding her close in his arms, cradling her on his heart, where there was nothing but a dumb, dull acceptance. The magnitude of this loss held a kernel of kindness, by stunning sorrow and blotting out time; but at last the jewelled dagger, falling from her hair to the floor, roused him. He bent, holding her in one arm, and while carefully replacing the bauble on the crest of the highest wave of her hair as she always wore it, remembered that evening by the fire in the glade when he had first replaced it thus, and the remembrance was as a turn of the knife in his wound.

As he moved, his eye was caught by a book lying on the divan near her hand, probably the last thing the living hand had held, — "Ibsen's Plays." It opened as he lifted it, and a little gold pencil rolled out; down the page ran faint marks. The play was "Ghosts." Some of the words were underscored, and Alderdyce read them painfully, half comprehendingly: "*Yes, it is sitting here, waiting; and it may break out any day, — at any moment.*" He re-read, roused to the meaning, and went on relentlessly, turning the page to find more marks. "*But when I got to know what had been the matter with me, then the dread came upon me raging and tearing.*"

As he read now he strained the slight body closer and closer to him; great drops stood on his brow, and he quivered as though each word were a lash. Had this been her life in these weeks, — this, when he thought he held and guarded her in soul and mind as closely as at this moment he held her body.

"*For it's so indescribably awful, you know. Oh, if it had been merely an ordinary mortal disease! For I'm not so afraid of death, though I should like to live as long as I can.*"

With a cry of agony, Alderdyce flung the book from him; he rocked his wife in his arms, drawing the drooping head closer on his shoulder, sheltering her face against his own. He had almost breathed for her, and yet the intangible soul had not been his; it had thought its separate thoughts, plunged into deeps which he shuddered to glance at, looked in the face of the lurking horror of which he had scarcely dared whisper the name, and at last dragged her body from his very arms. But not yet, — his for a short time yet.

There were footsteps in the court outside. Alderdyce could hear a man's voice and a woman's coquettish laugh; they paused at the door, and through it came echoes of a rude courtship, — the man's urging, the woman's light replies. Was there still marriage and giving in marriage in the world then, for such ending as this!

He knew that he had only to raise his voice and the quiet of the room would be broken by what he could not think of, — figures crowding in to take her from him; questions; each detail noted; all that he had learned with tears of blood known to a careless world; Conchita's name in every mouth.

The whole man rose in revolt; he raised himself, laying his burden tenderly back among the cushions, stooping once more to touch the sweet breathless lips with his own and to rearrange the pillow beneath her head, with a jealous care for her comfort, pitifully unnecessary.

With an effort he turned away and moved first to the door, examining it closely; the hasp was wrenched and the fastening bent and twisted, but he patiently worked all into place. His face was set with a dogged resolve as he went on with the work he had set himself. The copy of Ibsen, lying where it had been flung face down, came next, and he touched it as a noxious thing; he tore out the fluttering leaves that now told of a second tragedy, shredded them in the empty fireplace, then tore the backs apart, and set fire to the whole. A vague feeling that he had lived through this before came to him suddenly, then a memory of the time when he had saved this volume from this same destruction at Mr. Santillana's hands, and for what? Had the father seen some foreshadowing of this?

The maddening "perhaps" of life began its torturing work,—might he not have saved her then by a turn of his hand? He shook the weakening suggestion from him, and after one more searching glance about the chamber of death, opened the door that led into the outer world, carrying the fatal vial in his hand.

Then it all came,—the horror, the confused running to and fro, the physician's useless summons, the flying wheels of his carriage in the street, and his authoritative entrance, checking the startled questions which received no answer but stony silence from Alderdyce, who stood at the inner door of the studio guarding it. He stepped forward to meet the physician, holding out the empty vial.

"It is no use; she is quite dead," he said, in a flat, mechanical voice. "I gave her this by mistake."

The physician caught the vial from his hand. As he drew the stopper, Alderdyce, with a supreme effort, fastened his eyes keenly on his face, and saw the horror-stricken expression which crossed it soften to deepest commiseration as their eyes met; then a tension somewhere in his brain seemed to snap, a misty dimness settled down on his vision, in which the pitying face receded, gradually grew smaller, and faded away.

He knew also that another confusion was suddenly added in the room, that a little later alien hands touched his wife, from which he fiercely protected her until a troublesomely familiar voice, which he could not name, interfered, and gently bade him carry her himself. Lifting her in his arms, he felt his way across the court, up the stair, and there laid her on her own bed. After that he was only conscious of days and nights passing, and of being led through some ceremony; but in his weary effort to grasp its meaning the darkness descended wholly, — a total blackness. with no night or day.

Its first break was a footfall, heard always after the first time it reached his ear; it was like an echo of his own in their ceaseless wandering through the house, into the studio, and back through the court again. Gradually he grew to listen for the sound, to depend on it, — never in vain. Little by little the darkness focussed into a figure, sitting by his side in the gloom, rising with his rising, and moving with his movements. There were hands which placed a cup at his lips, and a voice that crept into his ear and reached his brain, stirring it painfully by its unceasing effort to rouse him to what he could not comprehend.

And at last Alderdyce looked up with seeing eyes into Mr. Santillana's face. He glanced about the room, and recognized his studio, Conchita's divan, and then all came crowding back.

"'Forever blessed or forever cursed,' you said, you remember; have you come to see the curse work?" he asked quietly.

"Anthony, my beloved son!" It was the same haunting voice and footstep; Alderdyce recognized them now.

"It has been you, then?" he asked dully. "So you

have not heard? I gave her the poison, and she is dead; I think it was a mistake."

There was no answer. Mr. Santillana's face was buried in his hands; when he drew them away, they were wet with tears.

"Do you still recognize me, Anthony?" he asked, rising and laying his hands on the bent shoulders. "Can you listen to what I must tell you sooner or later?"

Alderdyce raised a white face from which every trace of emotion seemed to have been wiped forever; nor was there any change as Mr. Santillana spoke.

The story told was short, though it contained the accumulated misery of generations. The awful curse of insanity had descended in the blood from father to son, from mother to daughter. Mr. Santillana's voice trembled as he hurried over the history of the days when he saw Conchita's mother fading from him, first in mind and then in body. He was watching Alderdyce closely, but not even a fleeting expression crossed the cold, death-like face. He told how the hope of saving Conchita had induced his taking her from her Spanish home, guarding her thus from any chance knowledge of the legacy which might be hers; and when her unexpected marriage allowed it, even separating her from himself and from any sight of his anxiety which might betray the secret to her.

"But all was in vain, as it was written. There was no eluding it. Anthony, if I dared tell you of the days of agony and scenes of horror which I have known, you might count yourself blessed in your grief."

Alderdyce listened listlessly. "What matter now?" he answered, turning away his hot, dry eyes.

Mr. Santillana looked at him with a growing anxiety in

his face; the lethargy which it seemed impossible to break was deepening again.

"There is one thing more which I must tell you," he said gently; "there is nothing in my child's life or death which I do not know. Anthony, your secret is mine also."

Alderdyce started violently, and looked up.

"I found this in my room when I came," Mr. Santillana went on; "read it."

He laid a bit of folded paper on the table before Alderdyce, who tore it open with shaking fingers. A dark flush spread over his white face as he saw Conchita's writing. The words were almost too incoherent for understanding; but the irresponsible pathos of the tender farewell knocked on his parched heart as Moses's rod on the rock in the wilderness, — the healing waters rushed forth in answer.

Mr. Santillana bent over the bowed head and shaken figure with a relief beyond words.

"Thank God, thank God," he murmured brokenly at last, adding more firmly, "for this and all his other mercies."

A gray morning by the seaside — the gray of the horizon merging into the gray of the sea, a small vessel beating painfully in sight of harbour, and a white line of breakers on the sand, a sky full of dusky, low-hanging clouds, save for a strip of angry yellow, the wind's cradle; all Nature threatening and presaging a rising storm — was the subject of an unfinished picture which stood on an easel in Alderdyce's studio.

The artist sat before it, too absorbed in his work to hear Mr. Santillana's entrance or to know when he paused at his side.

The older man stood looking down at the work and the worker with a sad yet not unhappy smile. The artist's face was thinner, and there were new lines there; but if sorrow's modelling knife had taken something from it, something also had been added. There were peace and strength in the interested face, and no unrest in the eagerness of the eyes. He looked up as Mr. Santillana laid his hand on his shoulder, and smiled at the approval he read in silence.

"Yes, it is wonderful; and yet but a memory," said Mr. Santillana, at last. "Why so vivid a one, Anthony?"

Alderdyce glanced up at the beautiful, wondering face of the Pandora above him.

"But a vivid memory," he repeated slowly; and the two men looked into each other's faces as comrades who did not need words.

THOMAS BATES'S COVENANT.

THOMAS BATES'S COVENANT.

"BOAT, Michael Kelly! Boat, boat, Michael Kelly!"

He was not a mountaineer; and his dress, severely simple yet distinctive, was unusual on the mountain-side. He was short of stature; his black hat had a stiff wide brim, his black coat was buttoned trimly to the throat, and he carried a neat leather satchel in his hand. As he stood on the river-bank in the moonlight, calling at regular intervals, a figure more out of keeping with the wild surroundings could not well be imagined. His name was Thomas Bates.

At last an answering cry came from the opposite shore, and a little later, a heavy, flat-bottomed boat slid out from the sharp line of shadow cast by the willow-trees growing thickly on the bank. The boatman, punting across the current, stood upright, and used his clumsy pole as only old river-men can.

The stranger walked to the water's edge and lifted his head, looking out from under the shadow of his hat. He wore gold-rimmed spectacles, and the brown eyes behind them were shrewd, kindly, and humorous.

"Friend," he called, "is thy name Michael Kelly?"

The man addressed leaned on his pole and surveyed

the wayfarer at leisure. "You 've said it," he answered laconically.

"I was told that thee would carry me across the river."

Michael Kelly shoved the boat to the shore, and held it against the current with the pole.

"And further," the calm voice went on, "I was told that thee would not be offended if I asked shelter for the night in thy house."

"Get in," Michael answered, "and hurry; the waters are a' pullin' on the pole."

The stranger looked up stream and down as they crossed. On either hand the scenery was superbly wild; the moonlight was brilliant, and the river full of strange, rushing, restless sounds. When they landed, Michael Kelly tied his boat under the willows and pointed up the bank.

"Will thee then take me in for the night?" said the stranger, pleasantly. "My name is Thomas; I wish to visit in this district to-morrow."

Michael nodded; he was a man of few words. "I guess the Mistis can rig yer up a bed somehow, Mr. Thomas," he replied.

Thomas Bates looked at the cabin which was Michael Kelly's home curiously as they approached. It was an unusual-looking building: the pointed roof lapped over at ends and hung down in long eaves at the sides; the cabin proper was as if snuffed out by the extinguishing cover.

"It seems that thy roof-tree has taken root and grown, Friend," said Mr. Bates.

He listened with interest as Michael laboriously explained how he had first built his cabin, and then bought the roof second-hand from a neighbour who was tearing down his old house.

"It don' fit too well," he ended; "but it 's better too big 'n too small."

"Yes; and thee finds room beneath it for the stranger," added Mr. Bates, as they entered.

The inside of the one-room cabin was clean and neat; the open rafters were hung with strings of onions and dried herbs, and the furniture was rough, with the exception of a high four-posted bed, and a huge old-fashioned clock, which was ticking noisily.

The old wife received the wanderer hospitably; her life was monotonous, and any break was welcome. The supper she provided was appetizing, and after the meal ended, the three sat over the blazing fire and talked together. It seemed that Mr. Bates said more than his companions, and yet when his bed of "comforts" and home-cured feather pillows was made up near the fireplace, and they separated for the night, — if separation it could be called, — his hosts still knew nothing of where he came from or what was his destination.

"What is thy occupation?" he had asked Michael; and under the kindly, shrewd questioning, Michael told of the mine on the mountain-side, which he knew as a mother knows her child. It had taken him his lifetime to learn it; but in an hour the mine on the mountain-side, in all its aspects, was Thomas Bates's also.

"And what is thy faith?" asked the guest. "And what is the faith of the miners generally?"

Michael shook his head; his wife answered, —

"The day after to-morrow will be the Sabbath, and you might ride ten miles over that way and over that, and over that and that, and hear no sound of the gospel anywhere."

Mr. Bates lowered his head and looked at her over his glasses.

"Is it possible!" he said slowly. "And the superintendent of thy mine is a gentleman and a Christian, thee says, Michael Kelly; and thee has not even a Sabbath-school for the little ones?"

Michael again shook his head. Mr. Bates sat with his hands on his knees, gazing thoughtfully into the embers.

"Friend," he said, turning to his hostess, "is thee not lonely here at times, with the Gospel ten miles away, and with no children? Or has thee children elsewhere?"

The woman did not reply, she bent over her knitting.

"My wife is as barren as these hills," said Michael, shortly.

Mr. Bates looked from one to the other in silence, his eyes resting kindly on the primitive mountain-woman, who felt her reproach.

"And can thee, an old miner, call these hills barren, Michael Kelly!" he said finally. "Nothing is barren that the Lord hath made. Mrs. Kelly, if thee will shake me up a bed somewhere, I should be glad to rest, I think; I have had a long day."

The old couple were soon fast asleep in the high-posted bed, but their guest lay wakeful on his pallet. The noisy old clock in the corner, aggressively marking the moments, disturbed his unaccustomed ears. Tack-tick-tack!—he could hear the sweep of the pendulum in the stillness. For a time he bore it patiently, but at last he would watch with it no longer; he rose softly, crept noiselessly across the floor toward the clock-case, turned the key in the long, narrow door, and opened it. The old clock was silent for the first time in years when Mr. Bates lay down again. Almost as his weary head touched the pillow the old woman in the four-posted bed roused with a start and sat up listening, her neck outstretched. Mr. Bates could hear her scrambling from the high frame to the floor; she was talking to herself as she groped her way to the clock, — that regular lullaby of years could not cease and she not feel it through her dreams.

The pendulum swung on again, and she scrambled back into her bed contented; but Mr. Bates lay staring up into the dim rafters with sleepless eyes. He gave up the contest. He could smell the aromatic herbs hanging above him, and tried to give to each its name. The clock worked on drearily, and he tossed restlessly as he heard it.

Presently he spoke in a reproving whisper: "Thomas, thee is wholly losing thy serenity." He lay still then, with his hands folded quietly on his breast. "Lord, if it is thy will that I should wake, 't is doubtless for a purpose."

The next morning when the old couple roused, the only trace of their late guest was a piece of silver lying on the table. Mr. Bates was already half-way up the mountain-side, satchel in hand. He was following a little footpath which led from the old miner's door upward; he thought he might safely trust its leading.

As he mounted, slowly but steadily, he looked about him thoughtfully, and at last paused on a little platform on the mountain-side, — a kind of natural clearing; from there he turned and looked back over the way he had come. The valley and river lay below, and on the farther shore the hills rose in a soft, curving line like a green horseshoe.

The practical eyes followed the line of the little path on the mountain-side, and saw how a road cut in its place might be as a key to the valley and river, and lead to the site where he stood. He examined the platform carefully in all its bearings, and stepped it off east, west, north, and south, entering the records in his note-book. Then turning again to the Horseshoe Hills, he stood watching the birth of the day. The sun, coming slowly up over the centre of the arch, was glorifying the hilltops; but the valley below still held, here and there, clinging white mists on its green sides. The air was full of the fresh odours of the moist woods and of the morning.

Thomas Bates stretched out his hands toward the horizon. "Lord, here will I build thee a tabernacle," he said aloud.

The young superintendent of the mine was trimming the vines on his veranda when he saw a strange figure walking up the road toward his gate.

As the superintendent advanced, the stranger spoke mildly: "I am Thomas Bates. I chanced to be in thy neighbourhood, and it was borne in upon me to visit the mine before returning to my home."

The superintendent flung open the gate quickly, and took the satchel from Mr. Bates's hand. "Will you come in, sir, and will you stay with us for a time?" he said. "Have you breakfasted yet, Mr. Bates?"

"I have not breakfasted, and I thank thee for thy thoughtfulness. This mountain air opens the heart as well as sharpens the appetite, it seems; I have met with kindness in the valley, also."

The superintendent installed his guest in the parlour, and sought his wife; he found her in the nursery. "My dear," he said, "let the children shift for themselves. Put on your apron, and get up a royal breakfast; the owner of the mine is in the parlour."

Before the day ended the superintendent was a very weary man, but he found time to thank his God that he had been an honest one. Had there been a dark corner to cover, the shaving of a penny to hide, he knew that those shrewd eyes would have picked out the fault unsparingly.

As Mr. Bates closed the last ledger opened for his inspection, he laid his hand on the pile of books, and looked musingly into his superintendent's face.

"Friend," he said, "I find my mine run economically and prudently. I find thy methods wise and thy books in order. Thee has in some cases followed thy own mind rather than instructions sent thee, but I perceive that it has been well; and the man who is able to separate good advice from bad stands in no need of advising. This for the material; and now what is the prevailing faith among thy miners?"

The superintendent did not know. "That had not come under his supervision," he said.

Mr. Bates gazed out of the office-window, from which he could see a part of the curve of the Horseshoe Hills.

"It may be as well to discover their wishes," he said. "To-morrow will be the Sabbath; and if thee will give it out among the miners to-night, I will speak to them on the subject in the afternoon. I presume thee will be willing to lend me thy rooms in which to meet them."

On Sunday afternoon, from the mountains piled up all around and from the valley below, the people came pouring in on foot and in carts.

The superintendent was standing on his veranda watching their approach, when Mr. Bates joined him.

"Does thee think that moving line on the hillside can be the miners?" asked the mine's owner.

"I am very sorry," answered the superintendent; "but I find that the people have gained a false impression of your calling them together. They think there is to be a service of some kind, you see, and they are drawing in from miles around."

Mr. Bates smiled. "Why should thee be sorry? It is not what I anticipated, but we will meet the occasion in some manner; the Bible is ever ready at hand, and thy wife has a sweet voice in singing. I heard her humming over the little one's cradle this morning. But I find that I must ask a favour of thee. Will thee drive me over to the railroad before nightfall? It is important that I take the early train in the morning, and I will spend the night with the station-master there. I put the hour of leaving the mine in thy hands."

Among the first arrivals were Michael Kelly and his wife; they stood staring at Mr. Bates, recognizing their late guest.

Mr. Bates received them warmly, stretching out a hand to each. "Mrs. Kelly, thee and thy husband are welcome as old friends," he said; "and I prophesy that the Gospel shall come nearer to thy dwelling by ten miles."

The superintendent's parlour and the veranda were crowded with men, women, and children when Mr. Bates rose and opened the meeting with prayer. He removed his stiff black hat and set it carefully on the chair behind him, before beginning the earnest petition for help and guidance.

The simple service consisted of alternate readings from the Scriptures, prayers, and familiar hymns led by the superintendent's wife.

Finally Mr. Bates lifted his hat from the chair and replaced it on his head.

"Friends," he said, "I have gathered you together for the purpose of consulting with you. I hold in my hand a list of the various Christian denominations, and as I read from it, I ask that those who belong to the denomination called will raise their hands. I mention, first, the Society of Friends."

A withered old woman at the back of the room held up a trembling hand alone. Mr. Bates looked over his glasses at the others, but none moved.

"Sister," he said quietly, "I am glad to have worshipped with thee; and now I mention Baptists."

A stray hand was raised here and there, and the list went on. "Methodists."

From every side, rising like a flight of trained pigeons at a given word, the hands flew up.

Mr. Bates folded the list and spoke, —

"Friends, I perceive that the Methodist persuasion is the faith most acceptable. There has been, up to this time, no meeting-house for worship in the community; for this I do not hold you responsible, but on my departure I will confer with the bishop on the matter. Providence permitting, there will be erected, at an early day, a suitable and substantial building for worship on the platform of land lying between Michael Kelly's cabin and the mine. The present path will then be converted into a useful roadway, also substantially laid; and both are for an inheritance for your children, and your children's children, and your children's children's children. And now I must not keep you longer from your homes; for many of them are distant, and the night will be falling, and I too have a journey before me; but before we separate, let us sing once more together, —

> "'God moves in a mysterious way,
> His wonders to perform.'"

During the singing the superintendent slipped away, and after a little the stable-boy made his way to Mr. Bates's side and whispered in his ear.

Mr. Bates rose and followed him from the room.

In the road outside stood a light buggy, and harnessed in it was the joy of the superintendent's heart.

He was himself standing at the restive mare's head, striving to subdue her vaulting ambition to walk on two legs as her master.

"I am afraid I must ask you to hurry a little," the superintendent began when Mr. Bates appeared; but the hint was unnecessary. Before he ended Mr. Bates was in the buggy, his hands twisted in the reins; his brown eyes were twinkling and shining behind his glasses as he looked down on the quivering beautiful back between the shafts.

"Thee had best leap in, Friend," said the calm voice; "I perceive that thy mare will not endure much foolishness."

The voices in the parlour died away before the last verse of the hymn ended. The singers were crowding out on the veranda, gaping at the back of the swaying buggy and the two figures it held. The shorter figure was grasping the reins in one strong hand, and holding the brim of his stiff black hat with the other.

To-day there stands on the platform which overlooks the valley and the Horseshoe Hills a stone church where regular services are held, and where the men, women, and children from the mountain, the valley, and the river come through rain and shine.

There is a roadway for them to follow, which was only indicated by a path before. And far down in the valley stands a little cabin with an overgrown roof, beneath which a noisy clock still marks the moments wheezingly, and Michael Kelly tells how the stone church came to be built on the platform.

I know them all.

MISS CHESILIA McCARTHY.

Miss Chesilia McCarthy.

"GOOD-MORNING, ladies, good-morning!" said the old doctor, baring his head and bowing low from his buggy. His young assistant, who was seated beside him, raised his hat and looked out also, but saw only an old-fashioned double house, set back from the street corner, with every door closed, and the windows sealed by green Venetian blinds.

"To whom did you speak, Dr. Johnstone?" he asked. "I see no one."

"Nor I; but they are there, nevertheless, — certainly one, possibly both. I always speak to them as I pass, — Miss Chesilia McCarthy at one window, and Miss Anne at the other. I mean to introduce you there before long. I'll take the reins now myself, if you please; I only wanted to watch you handle the sorrel. I never know a man until I see him with a horse, nor a woman until I see her with a man. You'll do; and it's the direct kindness of Providence that you will. I was as nervous about you as if I were choosing a wife. A man has to walk as delicately as Agag in this town."

Dr. Johnstone was in high good-humour; he had written to a professional brother to send him a crutch in his old age, and Dr. Jesse Taylor had been the reply.

Fortunately, the young doctor was as satisfied as the old one; though he, too, had known his anxious moments. He doubted the reception of his modern methods with these primitive minds; but it was not long before he discovered that he had only one man to please.

Dr. Johnstone had not brought all the rising generation of Belhaven into the world, and their parents before them, for nothing; from this vantage-ground the old autocrat issued his orders, and Belhaven would as soon have questioned the calling of Saint Paul to the apostleship as the ability of one on whom the seal of his approval was set.

Have you ever seen Belhaven, with its Princess Anne Street, its Royal George Street, its Duke of Gloucester Street, and its old houses with the flavour of nobility still clinging about them in this land of democracy?

Courtly gentlemen in knee-breeches and lace ruffles, and gracious ladies with their high heads powdered, rustling in brocade and dainty arrogance, equally versed in patching their pretty proud faces and the household linen, in handling the fan and the duster, might return to their homes there to-day and find all as familiar as in the old colonial times.

Perhaps the mistake lay in building the city too near the sleepy river, and the lapping water hushed it into drowsiness. However it may have happened, Belhaven stands a completed city, and is a village. Commerce has drifted down the Potomac and blessed a rival.

The quaintness resulting from the individuality of a city thus stamping the inhabitants, rather than the inhabitants the city, tickled Jesse Taylor's sense of humour, and the sweet, old-fashioned simplicity delighted his heart.

As he stood on the steps of the McCarthy mansion with

Dr. Johnstone, waiting to be admitted for his first call, he thought that he had never seen a house of death more jealously closed; yet when he had driven past alone earlier in the day, an unaccountable impulse had made him bow low from the buggy, after the manner of his chief, and it had seemed to him that two shadowy forms behind the green Venetian blinds inclined their heads in answer. There was an odd decoration on the McCarthy steps. Age had separated the stone slabs from each other, and the winds rushing up Princess Anne Street from the river had blown earth into the cracks until enough soil had collected to nourish some seeds of sweet alyssum which a vagrant breeze fancied planting there. From this small beginning the sweet white blossoms had taken possession of the old gray steps, spreading and spreading, crack by crack, flinging up a greeting of delicate perfume from their white heads in the faces of those who stepped over them to reach the door.

Jesse Taylor was deciding that he had never seen anything prettier or more characteristic of Belhaven, when a face at an open window of the house on the opposite corner, far prettier than any head of sweet alyssum, caught his eye. Before he had time to ask his companion the question which was on his lips, the door of the McCarthy mansion opened, and Dr. Taylor turned to see Amanda, sole remnant of the McCarthy retainers.

"How are the ladies, Amanda? Are they at home?" asked Dr. Johnstone.

A mere formula, — no one ever found the ladies McCarthy out; exercise was not considered necessary in their day. Amanda answered only the first question as she ushered the guests into the parlour.

"Miss Chesilia she ain' so well; she dun wash de bus' dis mawnin', ye' know."

"Yes, I know. Why in the world don't you do it for her, Amanda?"

"Me!" exclaimed the old negress, chuckling; "when she ain' even tressin' Miss Anne to tech it! She don' skercely tress me fur to stick de peens in de peencushion, nohow," she added, as she limped off.

In the dim light of the square parlour, the white-shrouded furniture seemed to Jesse Taylor as ghosts of departed sofas and chairs. He had time only to glance about him before Miss Anne McCarthy entered. She was like any one of a hundred other old ladies; but Miss Chesilia, who followed her with a soft, gliding step, the toe touching the floor first, was as unique as a bit of cherished porcelain.

It was evident that she was Dr. Johnstone's favourite. He held her hand in both of his as he bade her good-morning, calling her "My dear child." His hair was white, while hers was only gray, and still curled charmingly about her forehead and soft blue eyes. She had the eyes of a young girl, not an old woman; and they were the only large things about her, for she was of fairy-like proportions.

Dr. Taylor was charmed with Miss Chesilia, but he could not feel that his visit was a success in all respects; he was at cross purposes all through. While talking with Miss Anne he could give only half attention; the conversation on the other side of the room was more interesting by far.

"You know, Dr. Johnstone, I always wash dear father's bust on his birthday," Miss Chesilia was saying sadly, "and I simply prepare to feel ill afterwards; it seems so disrespectful. And to-day he looked so helpless, and oh! so sad, when the water trickled down his face and dripped off the end of his nose and ran into his ears, I said out loud, as if he could hear, 'Forgive me, dear father, forgive me.'"

"I know," answered the doctor, gently,—"I know. That's where we old bachelors lose, my dear child; when I leave this world somebody may take my bust out to the hydrant and pump on it or slap it clean with a duster, certainly no one will ever wash it with sacred tears."

And then Dr. Taylor, forcing himself back to his conversation with Miss Anne, asked a question which seemed to him innocent enough.

"Can you tell me who lives in the opposite house, Miss McCarthy?"

Miss Anne drew herself up, and glanced across the room at her sister.

Dr. Johnstone and Miss Chesilia stopped talking.

"The man who lives there," said Miss Anne, frigidly, "is named Birch,—Thomas Birch. His father was a butcher, and his grandfather also, I believe; was he not, Dr. Johnstone?"

The old doctor was knitting his brows. "Some desperate character of that kind, I believe, mem," he answered shortly.

His lady patients knew that the doctor was vexed when he called them "mem;" but Miss Anne went on agressively: "I think that Thomas Birch himself has left chops and ribs at our back door at times."

Dr. Johnstone was about to retort; but Miss Chesilia's

soft tones, softer by contrast, broke in. "Anne, suppose you bid Amanda bring some shrub and cake."

Dr. Johnstone's brow cleared. He loved Miss Chesilia, and he loved shrub. "I wish Congress over there would pass a law that callers should always be offered shrub on a hot day," he said.

So the little discomfort passed, and the visit ended pleasantly. But Miss Anne looked through the blinds into the street, and watched the two doctors walking away together; and it was not of them that she was thinking when she said bitterly,—

"In spite of all, you see, they are on the crest of the wave, Sister Chesilia."

Miss Chesilia, at the other window, glanced across at the opposite house. "No, Anne, no; or only as the foam is," she answered firmly.

Amanda, who was hobbling about clearing away the remains of the repast, now entered into the conversation as a member of the family, also in metaphor.

"'Deed now, I don' know, Miss Chesilia; 'pears to me like skim milk do git to rise above de cream in dese days. Fur me, I ain' believin' in people what ain' people a-settin' up to go wid people. Rich or po', I don' keer, jes' give me de fust quality."

"That will do, Amanda," said Miss Chesilia; but she sighed as she said it. The house across the way was very obvious every time she looked from the window; and a little figure, wonderfully like herself in past years, flitted in and out perpetually. Miss Chesilia loved freshness and youth, and she turned away with another sigh.

"Chesilia is the best woman in the world,—the very best," Dr. Johnstone was saying as he walked down the street. "If it had not been for Anne's nagging and that old witch Amanda, I could have stopped this nonsense about the opposite house long ago. I don't know though," he added honestly; "'Dear father' has more influence in his grave than I have out of it. You would think that bust a human being to hear her talk. Well, it is n't much harder than old Dennis McCarthy showed himself. That blood is as just as Aristides and as proud as Lucifer. He never forgave Sarah to the day of his death."

"Does Sarah live in the opposite house?" asked Dr. Taylor, with interest.

"No, Sarah went to her rest years ago; not before she had time to make it lively for her family, though."

"Then who does live there?"

"Anne told you. Thomas Birch, — butcher's boy. Sarah ran away and married him, when she found she could n't manage it in any other way. He was clever enough; I always liked the man. He struck out from here early, studied law, and made money, — plenty of it. Sarah met him somehow when he came home for a visit, and he took her away with him as Mrs. Birch. It would n't have been so bad if he had belonged to another city; Anne can't forget those chops and ribs at the back door. It was pretty hard on the McCarthys, and particularly so when he came back here to end his days after Sarah died. Amanda belonged to Sarah through an inheritance which Dennis McCarthy could n't cut off; but her mistress died and the slaves were freed, and Amanda came hobbling here to her old home and genteel poverty as fast as she could come. Tom Birch would have given his eyes to keep her. When you taste her fried chicken and mush, you'll see why. But it was no use, back she came. There was something fine in that though. With all his faults there is nothing shoddy about the negro; so the three old ladies live together, happily enough. Now you know the whole story."

"It was not Thomas Birch I saw at the window," said Dr. Taylor; "unless Thomas Birch is as slim as a peach switch in the fall, and as pretty as one in the spring."

The old doctor laughed. "Ah, no, that was n't Tom; that must have been Chessy. Sarah named her for Chesilia, as an olive branch; but olives were a taste not to be acquired by the McCarthy family. It was a sad affair, very sad; and the results have been unfortunate all around."

"Except Chessy," amended Dr. Taylor; "I would n't call Chessy an unfortunate result."

"Well, she has not had an easy time, either, poor child. People here have taken her up decidedly, but not those who ought to be most to her. I am taking you there now, by the way. Thank Heaven only the side of the house faces the McCarthy mansion! The front door opens on Royal George Street, around the corner. I should n't like to think that Chesilia was watching me every time I mounted these steps."

Thus introduced from house to house, it was not long before Jesse Taylor's figure was as familiar in the streets of Belhaven and at the bedsides of the inhabitants as Dr. Johnstone's. The summer passed away peacefully, one day telling another, with about the usual average of sickness and death; and then came the winter, and with it "la grippe."

At first the good people of Belhaven laughed over the epidemic, and said that Belhaven was in the height of the fashion at last; but after a little they stopped laughing.

The population was largely made up of those whose sands were nearly run; and to these came this new scourge, giving the hour-glass a jostle, and spilling the grains of time which might have flowed on smoothly and usefully for a few years yet.

Among the first victims was old Dr. Johnstone; and Jesse Taylor found himself called to the difficult post of adjusting an honoured prophet's mantle. And yet he was not called on suddenly. In the time given him he had learned many of the old doctor's methods, and acquired many of his habits; among others that of considering the ladies McCarthy, and particularly Miss Chesilia, as under his special charge, — and thanking Heaven that the house opposite opened around the corner.

Soon passing the footing of a parlour guest in the McCarthy mansion, it had become Dr. Taylor's custom to open the great front door — a locked door was an unknown idea in Belhaven — and walk to the foot of the stairway, calling up to "the ladies" for permission to ascend to the cosey sitting-room above, knowing as he did so that no announcement was needed, — they had already seen his approach through the green Venetian blinds.

In that sitting-room the numerous histories of the McCarthy family were gradually unfolded to him; and here also the holy of holies was finally opened for his inspection, — Miss Chesilia's tin box.

Dr. Taylor was familiar with the lives of most of those whose faded writing he was to see; but when Miss Chesilia lifted the lid of the case he felt that he was going through a species of solemn initiation.

Among the family documents were sedate and friendly letters from "young Colonel Washington," and others of later date and greater formality, bidding Dennis McCarthy to dinners of state at Mount Vernon. But prized above all was a worm-eaten silhouette of General Washington, "which he presented to my dear father with his own hands," said Miss Chesilia.

"But, dear Miss Chesilia, don't you think that you really owe these to the Mount Vernon collection?" Dr. Taylor ventured to ask. "They seem to me to belong to the country at large."

Miss Chesilia agreed with him; he was quite right, of course. Undoubtedly she was selfish in keeping them locked up in an old cracker-box in her wardrobe when they might do good to so many. And then she gathered the treasures together, and hid them away in the box, where Dr. Taylor knew they would continue to remain during her life, at least.

With much hesitation and some faded blushes Miss Chesilia pointed out to him also a spot on her soft cheek which had been pressed by the lips of Lafayette when he visited Belhaven in the year '24.

"I was only a little girl," Miss Chesilia hastened to explain; "but I remember the general passed up the street under a great arch and through a line of troops on King Street. One hundred young girls and one hundred boys lined the way on either side when he reached Royal George Street. The females were dressed in white with blue sashes and badges, and leghorn hats, and the boys in blue with pink sashes and badges. They were strewing flowers before him. My dear father always said that in sublimity and moral effect that ceremony surpassed all.

It was then that they led me forward, and bade me repeat some lines composed for the occasion. I can recall them now if you would care to hear them.

"'Fayette, friend of Washington!
Freedom's children greet thee here.
Fame for thee our hearts have won;
Flows for thee the grateful tear.
Loved and honoured nation's guest,
Long with us mayst thou remain;
Leave us when thou sink'st to rest,
Life eternal to obtain.

CHORUS.

''Happiness to-day is ours.
Strew, ye fair, his way with flowers!' *

My dear father said that General Lafayette seemed much affected. As I ended, he took me in his arms and gave me a most affectionate kiss just here."

And Miss Chesilia blushed again as she laid her dainty forefinger on the spot, looking so prettily conscious that Dr. Taylor longed to follow the illustrious general's example. He was as fond of Miss Chesilia as the old doctor had been; and as time went on he grew to feel that his day had not ended properly without a visit to her crowded in somewhere.

With the increase of the epidemic, visits of pleasure had to be dropped. Dr. Taylor had not seen Miss Chesilia for a week, when he received a note from her one day asking that he would call as soon as convenient. He hurried to the house anxiously, certain of finding her

---

* This poem and the description of Lafayette's visit are taken from records of the time.

struck down also; but she received him in her sitting-room, where she was sewing in her usual chair by the window, under the shadow of the white bust of old Dennis McCarthy.

Dr. Taylor thought she seemed nervous, and fancied that he caught a troubled, almost frightened look in her eyes, yet he did not think her looking ill. As she did not speak of her note, he would not hurry her; he began instead to praise the patrician features of the marble bust, — this he knew always gave her pleasure. Miss Chesilia's face brightened; she could talk for hours of "dear father."

Dr. Taylor sat patiently listening to her memories of her father's honourable pride and his strict probity. But he could not have been sent for to hear this!

Then Miss Chesilia inquired very particularly about Dr. Taylor's patients, or as particularly as he would permit, — for Dr. Taylor differed from Dr. Johnstone in this respect. The old doctor decided for himself as to how much of his patients' affairs was confidential, — and woe to him who complained! — but the young doctor repeated nothing of any kind. It happened that his most critical case at the time was that of an old gentleman named Ramsay, — Col. William Ramsay, — and when Miss Chesilia finally asked for him by name, Dr. Taylor was obliged to say that the colonel was a very ill man; and then he rose to go, in the hope of bringing Miss Chesilia to the point. Unquestionably he had not been sent for to discuss his practice.

Miss Chesilia rose also, laying a shaking hand in his, detaining him a moment to know "if there were many deaths." She seemed also about to call him back from the threshold, and then to change her mind. She did not refer to her note in any way; and as Dr. Taylor left the house and walked down the gray stone steps, where the white snow had taken the place of the white sweet alyssum, he was thoroughly perplexed. But that Miss Chesilia had needed him, for some reason which she was not ready to give, he was sure, and he determined she should not need in vain; as yet, he could go no further.

He looked over at the house opposite, and thought, regretfully and tenderly, of all that one of its inmates might be to her, could they be brought together; but as that was impossible, he turned to what had helped him more than once when perplexed. He tried to put Dr. Johnstone in his place, and to act as he might have acted.

The result was that, in spite of his press of work, Dr. Taylor paid a daily visit to the McCarthy mansion. Miss Chesilia accepted these visits with a pathetic if silent gratitude. She was restless and flurried in manner, and asked so many nervous questions about the condition of his "grippe" patients, and particularly of Colonel Ramsay, that Dr. Taylor feared she was laying herself open to the contagion through pure fear.

Still he would not force her confidence, and it was only when he saw that her secret, whatever it might be, was telling on her strength, that he determined to speak himself. On his next visit, therefore, he drew his chair close by Miss Chesilia's side, and asked her to shut her eyes and imagine him her old friend and physician come to visit her once more.

Miss Chesilia looked up quickly, but seeing that, although half laughing, he was really in earnest, she dropped her lids obediently, and leaned back in her chair with her hands clasped closely in her lap. Dr. Taylor could see that they trembled. He took them both, clasped as they were, in one of his.

"Now, if I were really your old friend, and not merely his messenger, Miss Chesilia," he said, "this is what I would be saying: 'My dear child, you are not treating me quite fairly. I am your physician and your old friend, but what can I do when you conceal your symptoms from me?—for that is what you are doing when you have something preying on your mind and refuse to tell me of it.'"

Miss Chesilia caught her hands from his and threw them up to her face.

"Oh, I never meant it,—I never meant it. Every year for the last twenty years I thought he would come back and let me tell him so, and now he can never come back; he is going to die, and he will never know. I had been sending him away for twelve years, and it never made any difference; he would ask me again the next year just the same, and then I would say no, and when he left I would follow him to the door and say, 'Colonel Ramsay, call again,' and it seemed to make everything all right. And then one night—I never knew how it happened—Anne called me, or Amanda was coming up the stair; but when I followed him to the door I forgot to say anything, and he closed the door and went out forever and ever. I knew just how he felt; I understood him so well. He would have come and come until to-day if he thought I wished it, but he would have died rather than intrude; and now he will never know."

Miss Chesilia sat with her face buried in her hands, and Jesse Taylor sat beside her in silence.

This, then, was her secret. If he were smiling a little, it was because he could not help it, and there was no unkindness in the smile. He was thinking of the lovely wife and mother she might have made, and of the sunshine she would have brought into the home of the gaunt, lonely man now lying silent and uncomplaining, nursed by hirelings. He could imagine what manner of man Colonel Ramsay had been in his youth. Now, the ruin of a Southern gentleman; then, stately and chivalrous,—a little stilted, perhaps. Yes, he would have died rather than intrude.

And Miss Chesilia, as charming and fresh and dainty as her opposite neighbour, tripping out of the square parlour after him, and following him to the door: "Colonel Ramsay, call again."

Dr. Taylor smiled irrepressibly; he could see the whole picture. "But could you not have let him know, Miss Chesilia?" he asked.

Miss Chesilia flushed as delicately as ever in her youth. She dried her eyes daintily; ladies were trained even to weep gracefully in her day. "It would not have been maidenly; he would not have understood," she whispered.

She went on, with more composure: "It was very hard for some years; and to-day it seems as if that time had all come back. We have never met since, except on the street; he would not annoy me. After a time I grew quite ill; that is, I was nervous and irritable. At first I thought it must be malaria, and I took quinine for it; and then, quite suddenly, one day I knew that it was nothing of the kind: it was only that I had grown into an old maid. That explained everything, you know, and I stopped worrying and was quite quiet again until now; but now it has all come back. It hurts me so to think that he will never know how it was."

Happily, in the relief of unburdening her heart, where

she had been for twenty years spinning over and over the romance of her life as a spider spins its web from itself, Miss Chesilia missed nothing in her listener's silence, nor noted his abstraction as he left her.

His thoughts had flown to the opposite house; he was thinking again how some one there would know what to say to her and how to comfort her. This conviction strengthened with him as the days went by and Miss Chesilia grew weaker; for she was weakening visibly, from no apparent cause, unless the depressing bulletins of Colonel Ramsay's condition might account for it. She rarely left her sofa now, and Dr. Taylor was far from satisfied with the nursing she received. Miss Anne was too nervous herself to be of use; and Amanda did not understand the case, and so did not believe in it.

The weather also was unfavourable, — a heated term, such as the South can offer in midwinter, warm, damp, and enervating, winding up in that uncanny phenomenon, a winter thunder-storm. It was in the midst of its tumult of wind and rain and thunder that Dr. Taylor came to the McCarthy mansion and first saw a way to the end he had in view.

He found Miss Chesilia lying on her sofa alone, weeping weakly. In answer to his indignant inquiries for the rest of the household she sobbed out that she herself had sent them away.

"Amanda broke off a large piece of a needle in her head when she was quite a child, Dr. Taylor, and it pains her terribly in thunder-storms unless she sits in the cellar; and Anne was so frightened I had to send her in to our next-door neighbour. She is a married woman, you know."

Dr. Taylor laughed before it was possible to prevent it. "Why, Miss Chesilia, does being married act as a lightning-rod?" he asked.

Miss Chesilia did not think that exactly; she could n't explain why it gave a sense of security, yet she could n't help feeling that it did.

Dr. Taylor laughed again; but at the same moment an inspiration seized him. "Miss Chesilia," he said, "would there be the same protection in a person engaged to be married?" He paused with a significant embarrassment; but no more was necessary.

Miss Chesilia was a true woman. The thunder was still growling and muttering overhead, and she was terribly afraid of it; but she sat up, clasping her two little hands together.

"Dr. Taylor, who is it?"

Dr. Taylor grew grave at once. "You do not know her, and she is not a Belhaven girl, Miss Chesilia; that is all I can tell you as yet. I must ask you to trust to my having chosen wisely; and, then, dear Miss Chesilia, I want to ask a favour of you, but it is so presumptuous I really do not dare."

After many assurances and much encouragement he did dare, however; and a letter was finally written, in Miss Chesilia's fine, shadowy hand-writing, which began, "My dear Unknown," and contained an urgent invitation to the McCarthy mansion "for so long a time as the dear Unknown would spare to an old woman."

"And you will promise to love her a little for my sake, Miss Chesilia?" asked Dr. Taylor, as he dropped the letter safely in his pocket.

Miss Chesilia could not promise too solemnly, or show

too much confidence. "Do not tell me her name, my dear, nor even of her home," she ended. "That you care for her is enough; I love her already."

When Miss Anne and Amanda returned from their respective hiding-places, it was to find Miss Chesilia no stronger in body, but buoyed up by the possession of a secret which they did not share. She would only tell them that a mysterious guest was to arrive the next day, and that the best bedroom and the fat of the land were to be in readiness for the advent. She insisted also on receiving the expected stranger alone, and when the appointed hour arrived lay on her sofa waiting with nervous impatience.

But when she heard Dr. Taylor's step on the stair it was almost too much; Miss Chesilia sat up, clasping her hands together, and burst into tears of excitement. On the other side of the door, meantime, Dr. Taylor was striving by every art to put courage into a poor little heart, fluttering even more than Miss Chesilia's.

At last the separating door swung open; and Miss Chesilia saw dimly that Dr. Taylor was urging a little figure forward until it had crossed the room and was kneeling timidly by the sofa.

Miss Chesilia wiped away her tears, and held out her arms, only to drop them again. It was Chessy Birch, who was looking up into her face with appealing eyes.

Miss Chesilia rose from her sofa, and stood erect and stiff, the colour mounting to her faded cheeks. She looked at Dr. Taylor; but he turned from her and lifted the trembling girl left kneeling alone before replying to the unspoken question.

"This is my future wife, Miss Chesilia; and you have promised me to be good to her."

Miss Chesilia hesitated; it was for a moment only. "Dr. Taylor," she said with grave dignity, "you are right to remind me. I might say that you should have been more open with me; but I have given you the word of a McCarthy, and the word of a McCarthy shall not be broken. My dear Dr. Taylor's wife is very welcome here."

But Chessy did not take the offered hand. She withdrew from her lover's arm, and her girlish figure was as erect and stately as her aunt's. Her blue eyes met Miss Chesilia's steadily; there was an answering flush on her cheeks. Was it the old McCarthy blood rising there also?

"Aunt McCarthy, I am not Dr. Taylor's wife, and I am your sister Sarah's child."

Miss Chesilia started. The slight figure, the blue eyes, the softly rounded lips and chin, had all appeared to her as the embodiment of her own youth come back in a vision. But although the hands might be the hands of Esau, the voice was the voice of Jacob; not thus had her lips ever ventured to speak in her gentle youth. She glanced across the room at the proud marble features of old Dennis McCarthy; it was his voice speaking in his daughter's child.

In the long silence Dr. Taylor was considering how best to retrace the false step he had taken, when a crash of falling glass broke the painful stillness.

In the doorway stood Amanda, with an empty tray in her hand; the refreshments it had held lay on the floor, and her rolling eyes stared over the wreck at the amazing sight of Chessy Birch in Miss Chesilia's own sitting-room. Behind Amanda stood Miss Anne, also rooted to the floor.

Miss Chesilia stepped forward; there was decision in the movement. She laid her hand on the young girl's shoulder.

"Amanda, this is your old master's own grandchild; our dear niece, Anne, and Dr. Taylor's promised wife."

It was an accomplished fact. The news ran like wildfire through Belhaven; the ladies McCarthy had acknowledged Chessy Birch, and Thomas Birch had once more called at the McCarthy mansion, — but it was up the gray stone steps and through the great front door this time. The McCarthys did nothing by halves. From day to day Dr. Taylor could see that Miss Chesilia leaned more and more on the strong young nature so ready to be her support; and it was not long before he discovered also that Miss Chesilia had selected a second confidante. One night as he walked down the dim hallway Chessy's light figure fluttered out from the square parlour, and followed him to the door. The light of the candle she held in her lifted hand fell on her mischievously solemn face and laughing eyes. As she reached his side, she paused to speak with the grave deliberation of a past generation, — "Dr. Taylor, call again."

Dr. Taylor, turning with a smothered laugh, caught the candle from her hand, and set it on the nearest table, replying as that faithful, modest lover should have replied to his mistress on the same spot twenty years before.

It appeared that Miss Chesilia had concealed nothing from either confidant, and they talked it all over in whispers by the light of the tallow dip, laughing a little, but deciding that there was nothing ridiculous in it, nothing ridiculous at all; the newness of their own love story made them tender of others. Before the consultation ended, they had reached two conclusions: first, Miss Chesilia and Colonel Ramsay must be brought together in some way; and second, that when the sweet alyssum bloomed out again on the old gray steps, Chessy should pass out over it in a gown as white as the blossoms.

To plan for the meeting of two lovers when one is nearing threescore years, and the other has long passed that sum, is not always easy; and before another week Dr. Taylor came to fear that the feet of these two faithful lovers were set in a road which was to lead them together, but in another land.

Colonel Ramsay grew weaker daily, and Miss Chesilia had soon to be moved from her sofa to her bed; for as his strength ebbed away, it seemed to draw hers after it. It was useless to attempt concealing Colonel Ramsay's condition; by some mysterious means, Miss Chesilia was always able to divine the truth, and sank as he sank.

Jesse Taylor almost believed that these two faithful souls, half loosened from the frail earthly tenements that held them apart, met together in the dim border-land between life and death, and held communion there.

"Chesilia" was the name ever on Colonel Ramsay's wandering lips, as was his on hers; only the added burden of her half-conscious cry was, "He will never know."

Chessy was sitting by her aunt's bedside, listening to this plaintive repetition, when Dr. Taylor at last brought her the whispered news that in another hour the colonel would know all the secrets that death could teach him.

Chessy listened gravely; and, as he ended, rose from her chair, signalling to him to take her place. She bent tenderly over the restless figure in the bed for a moment, and then left the room.

Dr. Taylor had time to wonder at her tarrying away so long, when she returned, dressed in hat and cloak. As he looked at her in astonishment, he saw that there were signs of recent tears on her face.

She moved close to the bedside, and spoke clearly and slowly: "Aunt Chesilia, Colonel Ramsay knows."

Miss Chesilia opened her eyes and looked up wonderingly.

Chessy went on: "He was restless and fevered as you are, and was calling for you over and over; but so soon as I came in he knew me quite well, and called me by name, — 'Chesilia — Chesilia McCarthy,' — for that was who I was then, you know, Aunt Chesilia. And I knelt down by him just as I am kneeling by you, and I took his hand just as I am taking yours, and I said clearly and slowly, as I am speaking to you now, 'Colonel Ramsay, call again;' and he understood perfectly, Aunt Chesilia. He lay very still, with my hand clasped in both of his, pressing it to his breast, with his eyes fastened on my face. That was the last thing he felt or heard or saw; for after a little his eyes closed, and he passed peacefully away."

Miss Chesilia's eyes closed slowly, and she too lay quiet and peaceful, passing away also, they thought; but it was not to be so. A new peace had come to her heart, and with it a new life. She was to live to see years of a married happiness that she might have known, to hear the old house echo with the merry voices and innocent laughter of children that might have been her own; and she was to find new loves and new hopes, — for to cherish an ideal which the actual has no power to blemish, is not to be unhappy.

And yet, when her time came, she was not unready to go. They had surrounded her with affection and tenderest care; but they knew well that she was ever looking forward to that meeting with her faithful lover, when they might be together in a land where no question of marriage and giving in marriage could enter to perplex and separate them as it had on earth.

"DIE, WHICH I WON'T!"

A Memory.

"DIE, WHICH I WON'T!"

A Memory.

"BUT am I going to die, Mother?"

"Why do you ask, my darling? Do you feel as if you were?"

"I don't know, Mother; I never died before. Father, you tell me."

"Nonsense!" said the physician; "of course you are not dying. Here, take your medicine like a good child, and get well."

Jere turned away fretfully. "No, I am not going to take any more; I am going to die."

"Take your medicine at once, my child," said a steady voice; and the boy, opening his lips mechanically, obeyed.

Mr. Barton followed the physician into the adjoining room. "Is there a chance?" he asked.

The doctor was looking grave and annoyed. "There was," he replied. "Who has been talking in the room? How has this idea taken hold of him?"

"No one has suggested it. Jere was always a precocious child, you know."

"Yes; but if we are going to have this restlessness and fear to fight as well, why, then—"

"There is no hope?"

"None. You may find means to soothe him; if not, —well, do what you can. I shall return shortly, for my part."

Jere looked down at his father's hands as they lay on the pillow near him. They were not so white or so soft or so small as his mother's, and the nails were not so pretty and pink; but he liked to feel them lift him about in the bed, and they refreshed him when they lay on his forehead. He moved now so that his cheek touched the back of one of them.

"There 's father hands and mother hands, is n't there?" he said. "Father, you 'll tell me the truth; am I going to die?"

Mr. Barton sat down on the side of the bed, and gathered his boy into his arm, lifting the hot, restless head upon his shoulder.

"Jere, you like to hear father's stories, don't you? I am going to tell you one."

"I used to like them when I was n't dying; I don't know now."

"A story of when I was a boy."

Jere nestled his forehead against his father's throat. "Lift up your head the littlest bit, Father; I like the feel of your beard."

Mrs. Barton rose quickly, and walked over to the window, looking out at a landscape which she did not see.

"When I was a boy—" began Mr. Barton.

"Yes, that 's the kind of story that 's best. Begin at the very beginning, Father."

"When I was a boy there was a great war going on; I am not going to tell you about that, though. My story is of one of its soldiers; and I don't think he knew much more of the rights and wrongs of it than you would."

"You did n't fight, Father?"

"No; I was very little older than you are. But one of the fiercest of the battle-fields was near our old homestead; and after the fight was over your grandfather, with all the men left on the farm, went out to help the wounded. The old country doctor went along, too, and I, although no one knew that at the time.

"It was a dark night. They had to go out with lanterns; and so I slipped through the door behind them, keeping in the shadow. I knew very well that I should be sent home, if they caught me; and I was wild to go. The first soldier they ran across was lying on his face. One of the men turned him over, and somebody held a lantern while the doctor examined him.

"'Dead,' said the doctor, with a nod.

"Then they all went on, I creeping after them softly. On my way I had to pass quite close by the dead soldier; and suddenly I nearly jumped out of my boots, for I thought I heard a moan. I was so frightened that my heart stood as still as I did; I can remember how it felt now. I did not know whether to rush on and get with my father and the lanterns, or to run back to my mother. Then I did neither, but walked over to the soldier's side, my heart going thump, thump, thump! When I got to him there was no doubt about it; I heard another moan. And this time I was too scared to run; but I yelled 'Father!' as loud as I could."

"Yes, that 's just what I would have done," said Jere; and his father drew him closer as he went on.

"My father and the doctor came running back. They were frightened, too, for they knew my voice.

"'What 's all this?' said the doctor; and then I told him that the man he had said was dead was not dead at all, that I had heard him moaning. The men came up with their lanterns, and the doctor made another examination. The soldier's leg was broken, and there was a big hole in his chest.

"'He 's as good as dead,' said the doctor. 'Here, Tom Barton, you scamper home; there are plenty of men on the field to save, and there 's no time to lose.'

"I cried very easily in those days if I were angry or troubled; and I cried then, and begged my father not to desert my soldier. At last he told me that he would leave one of the men with me, and I might stay by the soldier until he died.

"'He 's dead now, I believe,' said the doctor, flashing his lantern on the man's face.

"And as he spoke, the man opened his eyes, and said, quite distinctly, through his set teeth, '*Die, which I won't!*'

"The doctor burst out laughing. I thought it the most heartless thing I had ever known any one do. He knelt down again, however, opened the man's shirt, and stanched the blood oozing from the hole in his chest. The soldier's eyes had closed, and he was breathing painfully, with long rests between."

"Like I do sometimes?" asked Jere.

"No; worse than you ever do."

"Tell me how long he did n't breathe."

"No; I don't care about your trying it just now. Wait until you get stronger. The doctor gave me some stimulant, which he told me I might give the man from time to time, and then they went off.

"I sat down on the ground and took the soldier's head on my knee, every now and then wetting his lips as the doctor had showed me, and dripping some of the stuff between them."

The nurse came forward with the medicine, but Jere turned from her impatiently.

"You wet my lips with it, Father; and drip it in, like you did the man."

Mr. Barton took the cup, moistening the child's lips with the contents, and pouring the rest slowly down his throat.

"That was just the way, Father?"

"Yes, that was just the way."

"Then go on."

"When my father came back and found the soldier still breathing, he told me that the house was too full to take him in, but that I might have him carried to my old mammy's cabin if I chose, and that mammy and I might see what we could do. I followed the stretcher to the house, where my soldier was handed over into the doctor's hands. The night was already half gone, but I could n't sleep through the rest of it for thinking of him.

"Early in the morning I dressed myself, and went down to my father's study, where I got a big sheet of white paper, and printed on it, in great straggling letters, — I could not print so well as you do, although I was older, — '*Die, which I won't!*'

"As soon as my breakfast was over, I went down to mammy's cabin with the sheet in my hand, and pinned it securely on the foot-board of my soldier's bedstead with two of my mother's big bonnet-pins. When I turned around, the soldier's eyes were open, and he lay staring at me.

"I thought he was too ill to understand, for mammy said he was; but when the doctor came in and bent over him, my soldier was too weak to lift his hand, but with the slowest movement you ever saw he raised his finger and pointed to '*Die, which I won't!*'

"The doctor looked down at the foot-board and spelled the words out; then he looked at me. 'Well, you are a pair of you,' he said; and he burst out laughing again. I used to think the doctor the most heartless being that ever lived in those days; now I understand him, and I know how much better it is to laugh than to cry."

"Even when people are dying?"

"Yes; even when people are dying, if the laugh is the right kind.

"'You ought to be dead by rights,' said the doctor; 'but as you are not —'"

"Wait a minute, Father. Don't go on yet. I'd like one."

"One what, my boy?"

"A '*Die, which I won't!*'"

The figure at the window moved suddenly.

"What do you mean, my child?" asked Mr. Barton.

"I'd like one pinned on the foot of my bed like the man had."

There was silence for a moment, and when Mr. Barton spoke, his voice was unsteady. "Perhaps Mother will make one for you. Were you listening, dear?"

Mrs. Barton came forward. There were deep circles about her eyes; and her lips, as they set in a smile, were quivering. "Yes, I will make it," she said; and she went into the next room.

Jere tossed restlessly on his father's shoulder. "Mother 's so long," he complained.

But at last she came. She had a sheet of white paper in her hand; and on it, in great black letters, were the words, "*Die, which I won't!*"

Jere looked at it contentedly. "That 's right, is n't it, Father? What funny spotty paper you used, Mother; but it 's printed beautifully. Now pin it up for me just where he had it; tell them where, Father."

"Just at the foot of the bed, a little to the right."

The nurse pinned up the paper, and Jere read it slowly. "'*Die, which I won't!*'"

Mrs. Barton, with a catch in her breath and a quick movement, bent forward. Her husband stretched out his arm and drew her to him, whispering in her ear.

"Go on," said Jere. "Mother, you must n't interrupt."

Mrs. Barton went back to the window, and the story went on.

"My mother was very good to me; she used to excuse me from my lessons, and I spent long hours sitting by my soldier's bedside. 'You may learn your lesson there to-day,' she would say; but as she never gave me any book to take with me, I used to wonder what she meant. Now I understand that too. I had a kind of storehouse in my mind, where I kept things I did n't understand, and wondered over them."

"You understand everything now, Father, don't you?"

Mr. Barton looked down at the flushed face and listened to the quick breaths. His gray eyes, piercing and watchful, became full of unspeakable tenderness.

"No, not everything; there are some things which I shall never understand. I keep making additions to my storehouse."

Jere's eyes were fastened on the paper at the foot of the bed, then on his own hand; he was curling up the small fingers, save one which pointed to the foot-board.

There was a sobbing breath from the window, and the mother, now facing the room, hurried forward with an eager gesture. At a look from her husband, her arms fell, and she stood motionless, watching.

Mr. Barton's voice went on steadily. "At first I was sent from the room whenever the wounds were dressed; but after a little the doctor let me come in and hold things for him. Once when I was standing by the bedside, I saw my soldier's hand groping on the counterpane, and I put mine into it. After that I let mammy hold the things, while I held my soldier's hand instead; he would turn and look for it, if I were not quite ready. Every morning when I came in, I would point to the paper, and the soldier's finger would point also."

"Like mine does? See, Father!"

"Yes, just that way. It was a long time before he could speak, and longer before he could move hand or foot.

"'All depends upon being very careful,' the doctor said. He used to give me his instructions, and I watched my soldier to see that he did nothing which he was told not to do. I was very strict with him.

"'I believe the man is actually going to get well,' said the doctor, at last.

"And he did; but it was very slow. At first he was only allowed to sit up in bed for five minutes at a time;

I used to hold the watch. Then he got from the bed to a chair. After that there was no keeping him in the cabin; he would walk out with a stick in one hand, and the other hand resting on my shoulder. I suppose there was no prouder boy in the county than I when I walked my soldier as far as the house, and showed him to my father and mother."

"All well, Father?"

"Yes, well and strong."

Jere's eyes turned again to the foot of the bed. "What did he do with his paper?"

"What are you going to do with yours?"

"I would like to do whatever he did."

"The first day my soldier went out of that cabin-door we unpinned it, and he folded it up carefully, and put it in an inside pocket. He was going to take it to Lucy, he said."

"Who is L—Lucy?"

Mr. Barton looked down, his face changing suddenly. "Lucy is his wife now," he said slowly; "she was only his sweetheart then. She was waiting for him far away in the mountains. He told me all about her; she had no father or mother, and her aunt was not very good to her. My soldier was the only thing Lucy had on earth; he had promised that he would come back."

The nurse advanced again with the medicine in her hand. Mr. Barton motioned her away. His voice went on monotonously; what he was saying he did not himself know.

Jere's head lay heavily on his shoulder, his eyelashes rising and drooping slowly. Once his eyes fastened on the paper, and his lips moved.

Mrs. Barton, standing behind her husband with clasped hands, bent forward breathlessly.

"'Die, which I won't!'" murmured the childish voice; and the eyelids closed. The breath came softly and regularly through the parted lips.

Mr. Barton's voice faltered, and broke. His supporting arms and body remained motionless; but he raised his head until his eyes met those of his wife, and the overflowing thankfulness in them answered the question in hers.

Mrs. Barton covered her face with her hands; and the nurse, stepping forward, drew her gently away, her own eyes brimming over with tears.

"It is natural sleep," she whispered; "the crisis will pass."

THE END.

www.ingramcontent.com/pod-product-compliance
Lightning Source LLC
Chambersburg PA
CBHW021043030726
47496CB00006B/1661
* 9 7 8 3 7 4 4 7 4 8 4 8 3 *